KING COBRA

Also by Ward Greene
Cora Potts
Route 28
Ride the Nightmare
Desire in the Deep South

KING COBRA

WARD GREENE

CUTTING EDGE

ISBN-13: 978-1-957868-68-4

Published by
Cutting Edge Books
PO Box 8212
Calabasas, CA 91372
www.cuttingedgebooks.com

AN EXPLANATION

Although this narrative is entirely fictional and none of its characters is intended to portray exactly any person, living or dead, its truth is self-evident as a picture of what happened—and can happen again—in America when intolerance and persecution ride under the robe of patriotism.

FRANK DUDLEY

CHAPTER ONE

THERE WERE THOSE THREE, OLD DOC SLOAT, George X. Jones and Rosebud Boggs, and three trashier scalawags you couldn't hope to find at the time this story begins, which was not so long ago in Vesta, a city of the deep South. A drunkard, a cheap crook and a slut. Yet in a year they were rich, in another they were swindling or scaring half the United States and before the finish, when the money was rolling in so fast they couldn't spend it, they threatened to boss the church, the courts, Congress and the White House itself. And all because, I suppose, the human race is just childish and ornery enough to enjoy dressing up in bedsheets and picking on the other fellow.

In our town nobody ever called him anything but Old Doc Sloat, before the King Cobras and the Pythons and the Scorpions and the Eminent Cockatrices of forty states started kowtowing to him. We knew he wasn't a doctor of medicine or divinity or anything else, and we doubted he was a Sloat, the Sloats being an old and highly respected family in our town. He was just Old Doc Sloat, a "character," but no more important than Frogeye, the crazy nigger that sold soap, or half a dozen other local "characters."

He must have been a fine figure of a man once. He was over six feet, big-boned and not fat, and he had a voice like a bass fiddle. But drink had got him a good many years before he showed up in Vesta. When you saw the Doc at a distance, with that wide planter's hat aspraddle his ears and that long cane crooked over his arm—a "sword cane" he called it, though the man doesn't live that saw him draw—you might have been pardoned for believing him the sheriff, at least. But when he came close—well, I've known some sheriffs in my time as a reporter and none of them was a rose; and Doc outsmelled the lot of them. He gave off liquor and he gave off sweat and his clothes had a mossy odor all their own. Joe Briggs, our City Clerk, used to say that if the Doc unbuttoned his vest, a couple of bullbats would fly out. He looked, and smelled, dirty. And, likely as not, meeting you, his first remark would be an apology for the state of his "linen."

"My nigger," he would say, "my dadblamed nigger forgot to frill my shirts," and he would proceed with a cock-and-bull story about "firing the whole kit and bilin' of 'em off my place!" His nigger, like his "place," was as much a myth as his degrees from Harvard, Oxford, the Sorbonne and every other college he could remember the name of, but though everybody knew he slept nights on an old pool table in the basement of Scarlotti's saloon, his eloquence was so grand that you nearly believed him and all but forgave him his filth.

Oratory was the Doc's one talent and by it he managed to live. He could talk pretty well about almost anything, especially politics and religion, but he could talk damn fine about one thing and that was universal brotherhood. He had a speech on universal brotherhood he could deliver when he was so drunk he couldn't stand or spit.

"Man's inhumanity to man," he would begin, "makes countless millions mourn." He would trace man's inhumanity to man from Cain to the Kaiser, laying special emphasis on the Spanish inquisition, after which he would quote from the Book of Revelation and gallop off into the future. The Millennium, he would declare, is coming within our own lifetime—the lion and the lamb together—the unicorn and the winged hippogrif—the beasts and reptiles and peoples of the earth—at peace—at last—forever. And what, he would demand, will bring to pass this blessed consummation? "Simply this, brother—the proper understanding by superior minds of certain precious secrets I am about to unfold to you." Then, after a few gaudy references to the sanctity of womanhood, the purity of the home, the wrath of the Almighty and the glory of the Anglo-Saxon race, he would unfold the secrets.

When I first knew the Doc, the climax of this speech was an invitation to join the Ancient Order of Bisons. At various other times it was a bid to the Exalted Society of Knights Saracen, the Young Yeomen of the World, the Old and Established Order of Bears, the Nobles of the Purple Rose, or the AAA's, which, if you know your America, you will recognize as the Amalgamated Association of Artisans. For the Doc, as you have guessed, was by profession an organizer for secret societies.

That meant, down in our part of the world, nice pickings, for we are great joiners. The Elks and the Masons and the other big lodges run things pretty much their own way. You can't get very far in business or socially unless you belong to a lodge and many a fellow who depends on wide acquaintance for his trade, like the undertakers, belongs to ten or a dozen. And in addition to its general lodge-mindedness, Vesta had a special attraction for organizers at the time Doc Sloat was mooning around.

The state was dry, but the legislature passed an amendment to the law permitting members of bona fide clubs to keep liquor for their own use in lockers at their clubs. Of course, that opened the flood-gates. In Vesta we had more "locker clubs" than churches, some of them out-and-out saloons but most with secret order trimmings to make them "bona fide." We had Alligators, Buffaloes, Beavers, Cougars, Owls, Prairie Dogs, Wildcats and Yaks, with initiation fees ranging from a few dollars to mentioning "Joe's" name at the door. And Doc Sloat sold memberships and got drunk in blame near all of them.

He generally collected ten bucks a head for the national orders like the Young Yeomen and the AAA's. Five of this he could keep and five he was supposed to send to headquarters. He generally sent it, too, though it pained him to do it, for the Doc had sense enough not to kill the goose that laid the eggs. Occasional temptation overcoming him may explain his occasional switches from order to order.

He should have been able to buy a bath and a clean collar on his gleanings, but—five dollars, ten dollars, it all went down the Doc's throat, which gives you an idea of his capacity, with fair rye selling at a quarter a shot in those days and moonshine as low as a dollar a gallon.

When the Doc was anyways near sober, you could find him in Joe Briggs' office at the City Hall. The Hall was an old red brick building with sycamore trees around it at the edge of the sidewalk. The trees made it nice and shady, Joe's office was on a corner of the first floor overlooking Beauregard Street and the big statue of General Eli P. Manton. our state's hero of the Civil War, and all the politicians and wise boys hung out there.

Doc Sloat wasn't in a class with these elect.

"Some day," Joe would say, "I am going to kick that big bum right out of here on the seat of his pants—here he comes with a breath on him that would gag a buzzard."

But he never did kick him out. I think Joe liked Sloat and certainly he put up with him when aldermen would flee, sitting for hours, a lone audience to the Doc's maunderings. It was on one of those days that Doc Sloat revealed to Joe his big dream.

He came in wheezing and snuffling at the nose, a little soberer than usual, Joe said, but complaining because his asthma and hay fever and a bad cold had kept him up all night so that he hadn't had the heart, he moaned, to take off his clothes. It was mid-August and Sloat must have stunk vile, but Joe let him get away with his apology and a good chair and his feet in the window.

"I've got somethin'," said the Doc, and out of his inside coat pocket he dragged a fistful of papers all written over with ink.

"I wasn't surprised," said Joe, when he was telling me this a long time afterward. The O-R-R was a national bogey by then and the New York papers were wiring and sending correspondents down to scratch for anything they could get about it. "You see," he said, "Sloat was always springing some crazy scheme for reforming the world. They ran mostly to lodges since that was what he was mostly familiar with. He knew the rituals and passwords and preambles of dozens and he'd invented dozens more. I figure it griped him every time he made a collection and had to split it with the organization. He'd say to himself, 'Hell, there goes five of my ten dollars; if it was my lodge I could keep it all,' and he'd begin to study and fret. He showed me the prospectuses for a raft of lodges of his own—'Invisible Imps of Immanuel' was one, I remember, with three big eyes staring at you, and another was 'SSS,' Sons of the Sacred Serpent. He might have made them amount to something, too, for you got to hand it to the Doc; he knew history and mythology and all that stuff and he could sling some mighty fancy language, but the trouble was he never could save fifty dollars for a charter or stay sober long enough to file application. I always told him if I thought he had something good and advised him to go ahead with it—shucks, I was willing to see the old boy get along—and I told him so this time after he'd dug out his bale of handwritin' and plunked it down in front of me. But hell, I never guessed how good it was."

The writing Doc Sloat handed to Joe Briggs had been done on letter sheets of the old Merchants' Hotel. It began: RIGHT ROYAL AND VENERABLE ORDER OF RED RIDERS.

Now to understand why Joe Briggs was particularly impressed by this creation, you must know who the original Red Riders were and what they meant to us in our part of the world.

You've heard of the Ku Klux Klan, of course, and if you read an American newspaper in the 1920's, you heard of the Red Riders. But before Tom Dixon wrote "The Clansman" and Griffith made "The Birth of a Nation," the average American outside the South was pretty vague about the Klux. He knew they were something in history, but whether they helped Annie Laurie conquer Scotland or Cromwell win the Battle of Waterloo, he couldn't have told you to save his neck. And if you don't believe it, just ask the average American for any history he doesn't get in his daily paper. He was that way, in the early 1900's, about the Klan, and he was that way, in the early 1920's, about the Red Riders. Sure, he'd heard of the Red Riders—something in the Revolution, weren't they, or did they kill Custer?

Well, the Red Riders weren't quite that poorly remembered in our state. We had our part of the Civil War and we had our part of Reconstruction, and though, when I was a youngster, a good many years had passed since Union troops camped in my dad's cotton patch and burned the courthouse and left nicks you could still see in the big oak where they shot a man they said was a deserter, the War was a vivid heritage to every boy in the little southern town I was born in.

We roamed woods where old breastworks showed their humps under the pine needles, we found minnie balls and rusty bayonets in the fields, we recited Father Ryan's poetry and Henry Grady's speeches and we knew all about Lee and Stonewall Jackson and Stuart's cavalry and why the South never would have been licked if she hadn't been bled white first. We knew, too, long before the movies showed folks in Wisconsin and Illinois and Connecticut how it was, what the Confederate soldier faced when, "ragged, half-starved, heavy-hearted, with all lost save imperishable honor," he came back to his barren farm, his impoverished family and a horror a million times worse than the bitter taste of defeat.

In our state the carpetbaggers and the freed slaves made as black a hell for three years after the War as anywhere in Dixie. They ran the courts and the legislature and the railroads and the police, with Federal bayonets to back them, and they would have run the lives of white men and the beds of white women if they'd been let to. And who stopped them? Eli P. Manton and the Red Riders.

Over in the Carolinas it was the Ku Klux Klan, and in states farther west it was the Klan or the Whitecaps or some other form of vigilantes the desperate whites of the South were organizing everywhere. In our state it was the Riders. They came out of nowhere and they went back to nowhere when their job was done, but while they rode, they rode to a fare you well. A fiery serpent burning on a hilltop, the drum of horses' hooves in the night, red robes, the cobra hood and a hiss like a snake as the whip struck, and Mister Carpet-bagger went back in a hurry where he came from and Mister Nigger put out for the swamps. They weren't many, if the stories told were true, but they were enough to halt black tyranny and leave a white woman safe to walk from her front door to the springhouse without getting raped.

Don't think she didn't run the risk, either. You can find plenty of confirmation in the records or you can believe my Grandma Dudley, who swore she didn't sleep a night on her farm upstate without Grandpa Dudley's gun under the pillow. He was down at Vesta that summer, trying to get a grant from the legislature, and the stories he used to tell would turn your stomach. Blacks who couldn't read or write reared back in the Senate with their feet on the desks, yelling and hollering, cracking peanuts, staving in another barrel of whiskey, drinking champagne, smoking cigars and voting for any fool bill that came along, just so it gave them a grab at the public money to put it in their bellies or on the backs of their brown and yellow women that were sashaying through the State House and the Governor's Mansion with ostrich feathers and diamonds in their hair and a screech and a spit for any decent man or woman that dared cross them.

Oh, I know what they say about the South up North—we're just a bunch of barbarians that lynch niggers because we haven't got Sunday baseball. But please remember there are thousands of white folks alive in the South who saw with their own eyes their government, their homes, their world, actually in the hands of the blacks and the next time you go up to New York's Harlem, try that idea on your subconscious.

Anyway, I guess I've said enough to show why the mere name "Red Riders" meant something in our state. Eli P. Manton disbanded them in 1870. They say there was a grand roundup on top of Crag Mountain and they burned the fiery serpent for the last time and buried the robes and hoods and banners in a big cave. After that, the Riders ceased to exist except in people's memories. But they stuck there. When I was a kid we played "red riders" like other kids play cops and robbers and as late as 1910, all through that part of the South, you could scare a nigger to death by telling him the Red Riders were going to get him.

So, when Joe Briggs agreed with Doc Sloat that he "had something" on that sultry August day many years after the last Red Rider rode, you can understand why he was sincere. The wonder was, with all the locker clubs and regular lodges and Knights and Yeomen and whatnot parading every time they got the chance, nobody had thought to revive the Red Riders before.

"You ought to get a charter, Doc," said Joe Briggs, and the Doc, looking out at the great gray statue under the dust and the sparrows, lifted his right hand and swore, by the ghost of Eli P. Manton, that he would.

"To save the South, suh!" he declared. He didn't say from what.

Joe said he looked almost noble in that moment. "All he needed to be a Red Rider," said Joe, "was a horse."

But the Doc didn't have a horse. Worse than that, he didn't have a dime. So, for almost a year, the second coming of the Right Royal and Venerable Order of Red Riders marked time in the Doc's crumby pocket. It might have been there yet if it hadn't been for George X. Jones.

My first look at George X. Jones, I thought he was a humpback.

I was sitting at my typewriter in the city room, having come up the day before from Margana to take a job with the *Vesta Courier* on the strength of a year on the *Margana Star* and my dad's old friendship with Colonel Cronkhite, the *Courier's* owner. I was pretty green and scared and breaking my neck to write this story the city editor said was worth a paragraph, when this guy eased up behind me and said, "Your name Dudley?"

"Yes, sir," I said and turned around.

I never saw a face in my life that reminded me so much of a fox. You've heard the expression "foxy" and you've known people that were "foxy-looking"—well, George X. Jones was both of them, he was fox heart and hide. He had the red hair and long nose and red eyes of a fox, he laughed like a fox, kind of panting, and when he walked, he slunk. On top of that, though he wasn't tall, he carried himself stooped over so that he looked like a humpbacked fox, if there is such a thing. The heart part of him I'll come to later.

"The desk says you have a good story," he said to me, "about a man who got a permit to bury his leg."

I'd been sent to the City Hall to get the daily list of births and deaths from the Board of Health office and this certificate among the rest had struck me as odd. So I gave him the man's name and address and where the leg was going to be buried, in Calvary Cemetery, and then he started firing questions at me.

Was it the right leg or the left? Was the man diseased or did he lose the leg in an accident? Was he buying a casket for the leg and was he giving it a funeral? Maybe he was going to the cemetery with his leg to see it properly buried. What about a headstone—"Here lies my beloved leg, a better friend a man never had"—anything on that?

I had to tell him I didn't know, and I was feeling pretty chagrined over my good story, I can tell you, when he said, "Well, thanks anyway, bub," and eased away. The city editor hadn't thought to ask me those questions; George X. Jones did. I never will say that George X. Jones wasn't smart.

I didn't know who he was, then, or why he wanted my story—I figured he must be a big shot on the paper, the managing editor maybe, and I thought I had queered myself by being so dumb—but it didn't take me long to find out about him. Jones was telegraph editor; he had been a reporter for the *Blade,* our afternoon rival, and before that God knows. But working for the paper was just one of his jobs. On the side he was press-agent for half a dozen things, the Y.M.C.A., a couple of movie theaters, the local Anti-Saloon League, a dancing teacher and some churches. He wrote speeches for two or three politicians, helped edit a farm journal and corresponded for a New York paper. The reason he wanted my story was to include it in a city news service he got out for country weeklies. Most of the stuff he put in this, by the way, was plugs for his other clients. But Jones didn't last long on the *Courier.* He got fired; it was charged for selling tips on *Courier* stories to the *Blade.* I don't have to tell you a newspaper man can be guilty of no baser crime.

After that I used to see George X. Jones around town without thinking about him much. In fact, nobody thought much about him or much of him. The story of why he was fired got around and not even the *Blade* would hire him or take his press-agent stuff. I suppose he sent it in by mail in the names of the different organizations, for he seemed to keep busy and to have enough money to live on. But there wasn't a firm would cash his check or a man that would call him friend. He was just one of those smart, cheap crooks you sometimes find, I hate to admit, in the newspaper game.

You ran across George X. in places like the Delphi Club, which was one of the better locker clubs but a pretty lurid dive at that. The politicians went there and the labor bosses and the crooked lawyers and the black sheep of local society and young fellows who were trying to be rounders. The women were the phony-respectable kind that smelled like chippies and got insulted anywhere but on the dance-floor and in the bedroom. Once in a while a society girl risked her reputation for a thrill and less often you saw a known prostitute. Both classes were unwelcome in the Delphi Club.

George X. you always saw with a dame, pawing and kneeing her off in a corner, and the drunker and sloppier she was, the foxier he was grinning. He didn't drink—from fifteen to twenty Coca-Colas a day was George's allowance—and he didn't smoke. Some say he doped, but I never believed that—he was too smart for an addict. But George X. had his weakness. You've guessed it.

Mac Kelly, who roomed with him for a while when George first came to Vesta, said he never knew a guy who was so hot after women, who would go to more trouble to get one or was less particular about what he got. There was a redheaded dish-washer named Celia at the All-Night coffee shop. George hounded her for weeks. She wasn't interested and, besides, her hours began at sunset and didn't end till next morning—no schedule for romance. Finally, to get rid of him one night, she promised to meet him when she got off from work at six o'clock. She didn't show up, but George was too smart for her. He beat it, fast, to her boarding-house, and when Celia came dragging along in the dawn after twelve hours at the suds, there was George X. in the vestibule. He woke up Mac Kelly to brag about his conquest. I suppose the poor girl was too tired to hold out. She was one of the homeliest dames in shoe-leather.

Well, that was George X. Jones, a fool for love wherever he found it. He propositioned the waitress who served him his hot cakes and the manicurist in the barbershop while he was getting a shave. When he didn't have a date, Mac Kelly said, he'd pick up the telephone and try to date the operator. About the only ladies he didn't pursue for love were the ladies that sold it. That's why, if we'd thought about it, we might have been surprised to run into George the night we raised all the hell on Fern Street.

It was a Saturday night, a year or two after Jones had left the paper, and three of us, Mac Kelly, Joe Deadwyler and myself, were on the late shift. When we put the Sunday paper to bed at two o'clock, Kelly said he didn't want to go home and Deadwyler, who was married but had had a few drinks, said, All right, let's ramble. I was still a cub and naturally I was ready to go along.

The paper provided a truck Sunday mornings for reporters and printers who lived far out and had a hard time getting home after the street cars stopped running. The truck made one trip to the north side and another trip to the south side and got back in time to deliver the bundles of papers around town. It was already full of printers when we got downstairs.

"Get out," said Kelly. "A big story's broke over on Fern Street; we've got to get there quick." The printers grumbled, but they got out and Kelly said, "We'll be back in half an hour. Step on it, Pat."

Pat Hutchins, the driver, stepped on it and in ten minutes we zoomed into Fern Street and Mac told him to stop at Number Ninety-five.

Fern Street is one of those streets that used to have fine homes before the town started to spread north and east. Then the homes became cheap boarding-houses, with apartments built in between, and after Chief Walton put the red light district out of business, things got worse. The women scattered around town and in a few years they were saying you couldn't ring a doorbell on Fern Street and ask for Blanche without getting satisfaction.

Number Ninety-five was a big, gloomy apartment called The Dahlia. At that hour in the morning, when there wasn't another soul in sight and not a glimmer but the street-lamps, it looked forbidding.

"What's this here story?" Pat Hutchins said. "I've gotta get back and make my deliveries."

"The hell with your deliveries," Kelly told him. "You got all night to make 'em," and he went in and started ringing doorbells. We trailed along, and Pat Hutchins, too.

The first place we didn't get any answer and the second a drunk woman cursed us through the door and the third a scared-looking guy in a nightshirt said he didn't know anybody named Blanche or nobody named Thelma or Beatrice, either, and if we didn't leave he'd call the cops.

"We are the cops," said Mac Kelly and went up another flight. The first bell he rang he asked for Rose.

"I'm Rose," said this fat, blonde woman. "Oh, Henery darling, you are Henery, ain't you?" and she put her arms around Kelly's neck and began blubbering. He pushed her off and we all went in.

It was a handsome apartment, full of heavy furniture and low-lit lamps and rugs and bric-a-brac and pictures on the walls of "Romeo and Juliet" and the "Sailor's Farewell" and "Kittens at Play" and the "Death of Little Nell." The pictures were in gold frames and had the names underneath them.

The woman followed us into a big room, calling each one of us "Henery," but when Mac Kelly sat down and said, "How about a little drink, sweetheart?" she sobered right up and said whiskey was fifty cents a drink and beer a dollar a bottle. Kelly said we'd have four whiskeys and the woman went out and pretty soon a nigger maid came in with the drinks.

"How about this here story?" said Pat Hutchins, who was in a dirty undershirt and overalls and looked funny perched on the edge of one of those spindly chaise longues.

"There's no story, you damn fool," Kelly said. "Ain't you pleased and happy to be drinking with ladies and gentlemen in a first-class cat-house?"

"I don't see no ladies," said Pat, looking around, "and besides, I got to make my deliveries."

Kelly started telling him the ladies would arrive any minute and then a door in the back opened and George X. Jones, hump-backed and grinning as usual, walked in and said, "Hello, boys."

"Well, I'm a wolf," Kelly said. "What are you doing here?"

"Who—me? Why, I live here. This is my second home, ain't it, Mamma?" said George X. Jones to the blonde woman.

"Yes, Henery! Yes!" she cried and put her arms around him and began blubbering all over again.

After that, I forget everything that happened and it's just as well if I don't tell it. But we all must have got drunk except Jones. The truck was still standing outside when I left at daylight and I never did know whether Pat Hutchins made his deliveries or how those printers got home.

What I do remember—and what's important to tell—is George X. Jones sitting practically in this blowzy blonde's lap, calling her "Mamma" and "Rosy" and laughing like a fox that's fooled the dogs, while she petted him and Henery'd him and boohooed and the rest of us sat and watched them and got plastered. It was disgusting, if you like, but that's the way it was and that's the first look I had at Mrs. Rosebud Boggs.

I didn't see her again for a year. When I did, she was sitting in her own private office at a glass-top desk, wearing sables instead of a kimono, and as sober as Queen Mary.

Now let's get back for a minute to Doc Sloat. It was about the time of the Fern Street business, or maybe sooner or a little later, that he started getting thick with Jones. I don't know, as a matter of fact, whether the Doc hunted out Jones, hearing he was a smart fellow, or Jones went to the Doc, hearing about the Red Riders, or whether it was just one of those things that happens, but sometime that fall they must have formed a partnership, for in the winter following the state closed the Delphi Club and all the other locker clubs and it was in the Delphi Club that Jeff Broddy was drinking with Sloat and Jones when he heard them say what they said.

Jeff Broddy is a city detective, a plainclothes dick, and unless I'm very much mistaken, a Red Rider like plenty of other cops. He never would have told me about Sloat and Jones except I'd done him a lot of favors and he was a little liquored at the time.

He saw them, Jeff said, in a corner of the Delphi Club with their heads together, and he breezed over and offered to buy a drink. Jones didn't look any too pleased, but a drink was a drink to Sloat day or night, so Jeff sat down. Jones took a Coca-Cola and the Doc whiskey. When the stuff began to work in him, the Doc opened up. This time, as nearly as I could follow Jeff, he skipped over history and started right off the bat on the nigger problem, the Bolsheviki and the Pope. The Bolsheviki, he said, were plotting to blow up the Panama Canal and Wall Street and as far as Wall Street was concerned he didn't give a durn. But when they did, there was going to be a revolution in this country and the Catholics were the only people prepared for it. The Catholics had arsenals in the basement of every church, they were secretly drilling, when the Revolution came they were going to seize the government, put a Cardinal in the White House, arm the niggers and turn 'em loose on the South. But they hadn't figured on one man and that man was Simeon Sloat. He was going to save the country unless he was assassinated first, and if Jeff didn't believe him, he could ask his friend Jones there.

All the time the Doc was talking, Jones was trying to shush him up, grinning his panting grin but fidgety as a tomcat on a fence.

"What's the big idea, Doc, another secret order?" said Jeff.

"You are damn tootin' it's a secret order," said the Doc. "You are damn tootin', suh. And nobody but me knows the innermost mysteries."

"Hadn't you better keep your mouth shut if it's so secret?" said Jones.

The Doc piped down and Jeff said, kidding, "It takes money to start a lodge, don't it? Last time you started a lodge, Doc, you didn't have the dough. You asked me to loan you fifty bucks, remember? Sorry—but I done put all my money in Wall Street and I couldn't let you have a loan even to keep it from being blowed up!"

Jones broke in then.

"Don't worry," he said. "We got the money, ain't we, Doc? Or we know where we can get it!"

And with that, said Jeff, he busted out laughing like a hyena and neither one of them would say another word about the lodge.

When I looked up the charter of the Order of Red Riders a long time later, it bore the date of December third of that year, so I guess George X. Jones wasn't talking through his hat. The charterers were George X. Jones, Simeon Sloat and R. Boggs.

CHAPTER TWO

IT'S A FUNNY THING ABOUT THE SOUTH: IF YOU believed those editorial writers in New York and Chicago you'd think it was the most hidebound and intolerant part of the country and a Catholic, a Jew, a foreigner or anybody that wasn't a white Baptist or Methodist didn't have any more chance down here than a reformer in Tammany Hall. These editorial writers forget, until it suits their purpose, that the South is easy-going, and tolerance is a virtue of an easy-going people. It takes an up-and-coming Yankee to really run his neighbor's morals and cut his throat in business. If we have a problem like the Negro problem, we're inclined to let it alone till it festers in our face and then we make as short shrift as possible of the individual boil and let the problem alone some more. I suppose, if the North had the problem, they'd be more enterprising, even if they had to kill off the niggers wholesale as they did in Chicago in 1919.

You take the Catholics, for instance. I never knew there was prejudice against Irish Catholics in this country until I was almost grown and read a book about it. Seems that in the 'nineties they were really persecuted. Society snubbed them, Catholic boys and girls weren't asked to parties, a woman named Kelly had to take oath she was a Unitarian before she could teach school in Boston, busybodies broke into suspected neighbors' homes hunting nuns' veils, Grover Cleveland was asked to keep Catholic cadets out of West Point and it got so bad that many good Irishmen changed their names and there were jokes in the comic papers about O'Malleys becoming Minskys. And all of this, mind you, happened in the East and Middle West. So far as I ever heard, there never was a Catholic barred out of a school or a social club or a home in our state.

Of course, there was talk, like that foolishness Doc Sloat shot off about the Pope. Tom Watson's anti-Catholic paper circulated in our state in a scandalous, under-cover way and people got a shiver out of reading the shocking things that went on in monasteries and the cruelties that were practiced under the Inquisition in the old days. But they were mostly country people and if they believed St. Patrick's Cathedral hid cannon trained on Fifth Avenue, it didn't do any more harm than believing in witches. Most of them never had seen a Catholic, let alone persecuted one. In the cities, like Vesta and Margana, the Catholics had their churches and their schools, but they supported the public schools, too, and the hospitals and the community charities, and nobody thought of the Murphys and the Kellys as being any different from the Browns. If the neighbors read Tom Watson, they saw the Pope as a kind of far-off menace like Hitler, in no way related to the Flannagans across the street. Once in a while, if a Protestant boy wanted to marry a Catholic girl, there was a row because her family said the kids must be brought up Catholic, but if that's intolerance it seems to me the shoe's on the other foot. No Baptist mamma made her son-in-law swear he'd raise Baptists.

The Jews were the same way, except they were a little more clannish. They had their own clubs and their own social life and it was seldom you heard of a Jew being anywhere he wasn't welcome. Some of the biggest merchants and professional men in our towns were Jews. Their families were as old as anybody's, since before the Civil War, and I don't suppose they'd ever thought of changing their names or wanting to be anything but what they were, which was as cultured and generous and courteous a folk as you could find. As for the foreigners, we didn't have many. The Greeks ran restaurants and the Chinamen laundries and the Germans and the Italians and the Scandinavians, what there were of them, just faded into the general picture.

I notice I've been using the past tense as though this was a condition that didn't exist any more. It still does exist in the main, but it existed especially serenely in the first quarter of this century and when it was disturbed, as during the Leo Frank case in Georgia—Frank was a Jew convicted of the murder of a factory girl; he was lynched after a governor commuted his death sentence to life imprisonment—the fireworks were started from the North, where they know all about intolerance and aren't content to live and let live, or die and let die.

You may ask what all of this has to do with the backers of the Red Riders. It has a lot to do with them, for I want to make it plain that they weren't the great men of vision they claimed to be. If I am anywhere near right, the South, for all the sentimental tradition enjoyed by the old Red Riders in certain sections, was no hotbed of bigotry waiting a torch to burst ablaze. Sloat and Jones had no illusions about that. They believed they had an idea for a pretty good lodge and that's all they believed. It was bull luck more than brains when the Red Riders began to sweep the country. And the sweep, true to form, started in the North and West. Our state, the home stable, was the last to get excited.

The charter for the O-R-R went through the courts without a line being published—another secret order wasn't news with press-agents for dozens badgering the newspapers—and headquarters had been operating in Vesta for months before the average citizen had so much as heard of the O-R-R. The headquarters were on a downtown street. They were over an optician's shop. A sign hung out the window, "The Eyes of Kaa Are Upon You." If the average citizen noticed it, he thought the sign was the optician's and was advertising some new kind of glasses.

I asked Doc Sloat, "What is this Kaa?"

"Kaa, my boy, is the Hindu word for serpent, in particular the mighty python, and python itself derives from the Greek, meaning prophet. The ancients believed that Python was delivered by Gaea, the earth-goddess, who was also the mother of the Titans and the Cyclops, and that he spoke the oracles of Delphi until he was slain by Apollo on Mount Parnassus. Hence the significance of Kaa, the Imperial, who sees all, knows all and warns but once."

Then he went on at a great rate about the serpent in history, from the snake in the Garden of Eden—which really wasn't evil but the embodiment of wisdom, to hear him tell it—down through the sacred Egyptian asp and the Peruvian snake-gods to the King Cobra of India, the American moccasin, lizards, tarantulas, scorpions and salamanders. The human race, he said, has always worshiped the serpent and feared the serpent, and the serpent, more than any living thing, represents the beauty and terror and mystery that lie between man and his destiny.

I didn't believe a word he said and you don't have to, either.

This was sometime after the eyes of Kaa had been staring down on the populace of Vesta and a few days after I started working for the Red Riders. I'll have to explain how that came about.

One day George X. Jones called me up and asked me to drop in to see him and that afternoon I did, in the office over the optician's. It was one of the busiest places I'd ever hit, with a swell-looking gal at the reception desk and a big room full of more lookers at typewriters and adding machines, with doors leading to other rooms and in one of these, all fitted up with mahogany furniture, George X. Jones in a swivel chair and the best looker in the lot taking his dictation. I can tell you I was surprised.

He asked me to sit down and then he sent the girl out and locked the door and peeked out the window and drew the shade before he sat down himself.

"Look here," he said, and for once he wasn't grinning, "you're a man of character, patriotism and intelligence."

"If you say so, all right," I said.

"You believe in white supremacy, don't you?"

"Sure."

"You believe in the Constitution of the United States."

"Why not?"

"You'd get down on your knees and take an oath to support it and swear allegiance to the American flag, wouldn't you?"

"Look here," I said, "what is this all about? Because if you're asking me to join something, I can give you the answer right now. It's 'no.' "

The grin began to come back to George X. Jones' face and the red into his eyes.

"Well, it is something like that," he said. "Have you ever heard of the Red Riders?"

"Of course. They ran the carpetbaggers out and licked the niggers after the Civil War."

"That's right. And did you know there was an Order of Red Riders still in existence and growing stronger every day?"

"I'd heard something about it."

"Where?" he said, quick as a flash.

"Oh, I don't know. Some of the boys were talking. I think one of the printers had your literature, if it is your literature."

"It is," said Jones. "That's what I'm asking you to join—the Right Royal and Venerable Order of Red Riders—founded to perpetuate the bravest band in history—the brightest heritage the race is heir to—and we'll arrange to remit your initiation fee and your dues in return for a little writing."

I grinned back at him and shook my head.

"Nothing doing. I joined a college fraternity once and before that they roped me into the Methodist Church. But I swore I'd never join anything else. Besides, since when have reporters around this town written press-agent stuff for nothing?"

A year before I wouldn't have had the nerve or sense to talk to him like that. But I'd come along on the paper, I was known as a good writer and I'd picked up a trick or two on the art of earning money. If Jones wanted to hand me an extra job and the paper didn't object, let him come across. He did.

"All right—I guess it don't make much difference if you're a Red Rider or not. What we need right now is a writer, not a Rider." He was all foxy and happy again. "Fact is, things are breaking so fast around here I haven't time to do the writing."

The upshot was that I was hired, at thirty dollars a week, to come in three afternoons a week and pound a typewriter in the "crypt of propagation." That's what they called their public-ity department. They had special names for everything and they were the damnedest collection of names you ever saw.

The first afternoon they handed me a bunch of letter-heads. This is what I looked at:

Fearless—Faithful—Ruthless—Impenetrable
First for America and for Americans First!
Perpetuating the bravest band in history and
the brightest heritage the race is heir to
The Veiled Legion of
THE RIGHT ROYAL AND VENERABLE ORDER
OF RED RIDERS
Inc.

In the left corner of the page and in the right corner were ding-bats like those spectacles on cobras' hoods. In the middle, inter-twined with the name of the order, was a picture in black and red of a man on a horse. At least, you took for granted it was a man. He had on a red robe down to his heels and a red hood over his head. The cobra spectacles were visible on the hood. The horse was black, with red fire shooting out of its nose.

At the side of the page, in the place for the date, was "Grand Crypt of the Supreme Serpent, Palace of the Imperial Python." At the bottom of the page, in small letters, was "Cum clab ad Clastra."

I supposed this was Latin, but once, when I tried to trans-late it with a Latin grammar, I couldn't make heads or tails of it. I asked Jones what it meant and he grinned and said, "Ask the Doc," and I asked the Doc and he said "Cum clab ad Clastra" was derived from ancient Medean, but he couldn't tell me the mean-ing because it was a secret of the Order.

The Doc was Supreme Serpent of the Red Riders and Jones was Imperial Python—there was no secret about that. There was about the other officers. I found out, eventually, who some of them were—and so did the world—but in the beginning, about all the information I got was the general idea.

Here was the layout. They had divided the whole United States, on paper, into Jungles, Dens and Lairs. The Jungles were big slices of territory, like New England, the Dens were the states and the Lairs were separate bands of Red Riders in different com-munities. For instance, Vesta Lair was in the Den of our state in the Jungle of the Southeast. At the head of each Jungle was a Dread Scorpion, at the head of each Den a Terrible Tarantula and at the head of each Lair a Cobra. Every Lair had its own set of officers, the Serpent, the Python, the Cockatrice, the Hydra, the Basilisk and half a dozen others. Headquarters, besides the Supreme Serpent and the Imperial Python, had a Supreme Scorpion, an Imperial Tarantula, an Eminent Cockatrice, a Brilliant Basilisk and a few more supremes and imperials. I figured these were simply names for president, vice-president, secretary, treasurer and so on.

There was one other important office in the Riders—King Cobra. They were the boys who brought in the money, traveling salesmen who peddled memberships at ten dollars a head, kept four dollars, turned over one dollar to the Terrible Tarantulas in charge of the states and sent five dollars to the Supreme Treasury in Vesta.

My job was pretty easy. In the main it was writing letters and "literature" about the ideals and aims of the Red Riders. The literature was a lot of guff about liberty, fraternity, one hundred per cent Americanism and the practice of a thing called "blood brotherness."

"Blood brotherness" was an invention of the Doc's. It meant, under a lot of fancy language, that a Red Rider swore deathless devotion to his Supreme Serpent and loyalty to any other Rider in a jam, murder included.

The letters were come-ons to a sucker list compiled from rosters of fraternal and patriotic orders. Jones and Sloat figured, "Once a joiner, always a joiner," and they went to a lot of trouble to get the membership lists of everything they could, from the Sons of Confederate Veterans to the barbers' union. A sample letter:

"My Dear Sir:

"At the suggestion of one of your dearest friends, we are mailing you under separate cover the confidential codus of the Order of Red Riders, setting forth the aims of this famous secret society as revived by a cabal of leading American patriots.

"Your friend says you are 100 PER CENT AMERICAN. *No other brand of citizen can qualify as a Red Rider.* If you are interested, please fill in the enclosed questionnaire and mail it to the Supreme Palace. Arrangements will be made for you to meet a high representative of the Order.

"If you are *not* interested, it is best to *destroy this!*

"Cordially yours,

"KAA."

You'd be surprised at the number of one hundred per cent Americans who bit. Jones claimed a response of better than half. The combination of mystery and flattery did the work, and I reckon the implied threat at the end helped more than it hurt.

Sometimes Jones gave me my assignments and sometimes the Doc did. The Doc, especially when he was half crocked, could talk his stuff swell but had trouble getting it down on paper because his hand shook. He was fond of issuing "proclamations" and it was up to me, after he had ranted awhile, to whip them into shape.

A proclamation would start, "To All King Cobras, Dreaded Scorpions, Terrible Tarantulas, Eminent Cockatrices, Serpents, Pythons, Cobras, Hydras, Basilisks, Dragons, Asps, Sepsi, Dipsa, and Ophi, in your Jungles, Dens and Lairs, Greetings!" The Doc would then proclaim for about four paragraphs that he was feeling fine, the country was safe, but dangerous forces were at work and the boys had better get busy with more recruits if they wanted to protect their homes and their hearthstones. He always wound up his proclamations, "Officially uttered, inscribed, sealed, communicated and committed on this baleful day of the woeful week of the sinister month of the Red Rider year LVI; by the blood of our Fathers and the Awful Oath of our Future, Yours in the Unfailing Bond of Boa, Simeon Sloat, Supreme Serpent."

He had seven "b" adjectives for the days of the week, "bloody, baleful, baffling, bleak, burning, brooding and barren," and five "w" adjectives for the weeks, "woeful, weeping, wailing, wild and weird." When he got to the months he used up his supply of alliterating adjectives and broke out into "hideous, frightful, appalling, gloomy" and a lot more. I had to memorize the whole list.

Occasionally Jones had me write a "news story" he sent out to papers all over the country. This was usually about a band of Red Riders that appeared suddenly at a country church, marched down the aisle in their red robes and cobra hoods and silently handed the preacher an envelope. When the preacher opened the envelope after they'd vanished, he found fifty dollars and a printed card, "We have watched the good work you are doing and approve." The card was signed "O-R-R." Sometimes it was signed "Boa" or "The All-Seeing Eye of Kaa" or just "The Veiled Legion."

I don't know if the stories were true or if Jones made them up, using phony names for the towns and the churches and the preachers. He explained that "we are a Christian and benevolent institution and want to help the church, especially the Protestant church. And of course," he grinned, "we want to help the Red Riders."

He knew darn well that when those little stories got into print—and frequently they did, for they must have struck plenty of editors as novel and interesting—the readers were curious about the mysterious robed band, and sympathetic to the little old preacher who got fifty dollars out of nowhere, and if any of them received a come-on letter after that, they said to themselves, "Why, that must be the thing I was reading about in the newspapers; it sounds like an exciting thing and a fine thing and I'd like to join it."

I've said before that George X. Jones was smart. But even he, a publicity expert, wasn't smart enough, at first, to realize what publicity could do for him. Except for those squibs about the churches, he was afraid of newspapers.

"We're a secret order," he would say, "and that's what attracts the customers, secrecy and mystery. If we start rushing into print every time we charter a Lair or hold a Reptilon"—that was the name for a convention—"there won't be any secrecy left and a man might as well go out and join a golf club or a Sunday-school." And when Terry Mason came around and said he wanted to get a picture of the Red Riders, Jones told him nothing doing.

Terry Mason was a free-lance photographer who sold his stuff to the local papers and to big papers in New York and moving pictures to the people that make the news-reels. He was one of the smartest photographers I ever heard of. When there wasn't any news to take pictures of, Terry made news. He was the guy that took a picture at our zoo of the keeper pulling the elephant's tooth. Of course, no such thing happened, but that picture was published all over the country and zoo-keepers and many dentists wrote in for details.

Terry had a letter from the *New York Sphere,* enclosing a clipping. The clipping was dated "Vesta" and said the congregation of Rockdale Church, "near here," was surprised Sunday evening by the entry of a band of robed, masked men who handed the preacher an envelope and walked out without a word. In the envelope was a fifty-dollar bill and a note signed, "We ride by night." The *Sphere* said it had heard the old Red Riders were being revived in parts of the South and maybe this was them and maybe there was a good picture in it.

"I never heard of this church and I can't find Rockdale on the map," said Terry, "but this is headquarters for the Red Riders, ain't it? How about arranging a snap of an initiation?"

Jones laughed at him.

"You're crazy. This is the Supreme Palace of the Venerable Order of Red Riders, all right, but we're a secret society. We can't have pictures of our members in the newspapers."

"Why not?" said Terry. "They're all covered up with masks and robes, ain't they?"

"Nothing doin'," said Jones. "And besides, I never heard of any Red Riders parading around at night. That must be some other outfit. Local Whitecaps, perhaps."

Terry knew he was lying, and I told Terry he was lying the next time I saw him. He winked at me.

"I got my picture just the same."

"How?" I said, and he told me.

About a month later the New York Sphere comes out with a double-page spread of a dozen weird figures grouped around a wriggling brand burning on top of a long pole. They had on robes from their shoulders to their heels and over their heads hoods with the cobra spectacles on them. The caption under the picture was a honey.

"Days of Southern Chivalry Revived," it said. "The famous Red Riders of Reconstruction are being reorganized throughout Dixie by their founders' descendants. Exclusive photograph shows an initiation beneath the fiery serpent, symbol of the old order. Identity of Riders is secret, but they are known to be among the leading sons of the New South."

That afternoon, when I reached the Palace, Jones had the Sphere's rotogravure section on his desk. He was tickled, mad and a little worried.

"Look at that," he said. "It's a fake!"

"How do you know it's a fake?"

"No Red Riders would dare. Every Lair is under positive instructions to lay off publicity. If those are real Red Riders, they'll get their charter revoked."

"Well, suppose it is a fake—how are you going to prove it? It looks real enough to me."

"That's what worries me. Where did he get those robes and that serpent? Where did he hear about them? Somebody's been telling tales out of school."

"Meaning Terry and meaning me, huh? Be yourself. He got 'em where you got your stuff—out of the public library. Any fool can find pictures of a Red Rider in a history of the South. And any fool can buy some cheesecloth and draw cobra spectacles on it."

That held him for a minute.

"But who did he get to pose? Those aren't dummies."

"I'll tell you who he got to pose," I said, "just like he told me. Where would you go around here to find ten men to put on a bedsheet for ten cents? Those are niggers under those robes."

He stared at me like he didn't believe it and then he commenced to laugh. He laughed for five minutes and then he would look at the picture again and reread the caption and laugh some more. "Sons of the New South—oh, boy!"

But then and there he learned something. He bought a thousand prints of that picture from Terry and he had Terry take plenty more, of Red Riders on horses and Red Riders parading and the Supreme Serpent, in a black robe, standing with drawn scimitar before the Sacred Ophic Altar on top of Crag Mountain. They were real Riders, too, and not shines.

The pictures were sent to papers from coast to coast and most papers printed them and it wasn't long before every man, woman and child in the United States had heard of the Red Riders and was curious and impressed.

That's when the ball began to roll.

You'd think, wouldn't you, that the average American, being a hard-working citizen with not much ambition for anything except to keep his job and raise his family and pay the install-ments on his car and enjoy a movie or a poker game once a week, would be too busy to study the sort of rigmarole I've described and too hard-headed to fall for it? But I guess he's actually a cra-zier breed of cat than that little fellow in the cartoons labeled "common people."

Maybe it's childishness and maybe it's meanness and maybe he wants to get away from the wife and set himself above his womenfolks—"escape complex" and "will to power," I suppose the psychologists would call it—and maybe he really has burning in him the dim wish to uplift himself and find the answer to the troubling mystery of life. Whatever it is, he's got it in his bones to be one of the tribe with the big chiefs and the witch-doctors.

I don't mean just the rank and file American, either. If you've ever seen a national Shrine convention, with the nobles in their red fezzes and the bands playing and the patrols marching by in their zouave costumes and their arab costumes and their templar costumes under the cheers and torchlights and electric fire, you've maybe told yourself that it was a lot of foolishness for grown men to dress up and act that way. But you got a thrill, too. And when you think that Shriners are mostly bankers and judges and kingpins of business and industry, you can understand why the little fellow wants his parades, too, and his grips and passwords and rituals and secrets he can't tell at home because women are feeble-minded about such things.

I remember how serious we were at college about fraternities. I lay awake nights in my freshman year agonizing over whether I should go *SAE* or *Chi Phi,* and when my uncle in Vesta sent me a telegram, "Don't do anything till I see you," and I met him at the train and he told me my whole future might be ruined if I didn't join the SAE's, I believed him and Bill Crump cried when I told him my decision. Bill was my roommate and had already pledged himself Chi Phi. If it wasn't for men like my uncle, lodges couldn't exist and the country, I reckon, would go to hell.

But something happened in my senior year to shake my faith in fraternities and the whole secret order idea. A big, gawky freshman came up from the wiregrass and immediately got to be the butt of the campus. You know how those things are. There was nothing the matter with this bird except he wore funny clothes and knew all the wrong answers and believed anything you told him. He was really a simple, sweet fellow. And nobody really meant any harm when they kidded him and hazed him and played fool pranks like sending him to the Dean for the key to the absolute.

Jenkins didn't seem to mind being kidded. He was crazy about college and crazy about the fellows and, among other things, he was crazy to join a fraternity. So they initiated him into the U-Ama-Sappas, which they told him was the most powerful and secret frat on the campus. They clowned him all over town and gave him a cardboard button—"till your regular pin comes"—and beat the tar out of him in a "thirty-third degree." But Jenkins took it all seriously. He was proud and happy and grateful for twenty-four hours and did every fool thing they ordered him to and wore his button to chapel and classes and in bed and even when he took a bath. Then somebody must have wised him up, for they cut down his body next morning in Green's Gulch. He still wore his cardboard button, but he'd changed it to read, "I am a sap."

I've never been a very good brother since then nor any kind of a joiner. "Fraternity" may be a fine idea; I don't like it.

But there's no doubt that most Americans disagree with me. The Red Riders proved that. Within a week after Terry's pictures began to circulate, the supreme reptiles were the busiest snakes that ever heard the chink of a dollar. They were putting more

King Cobras on the payroll every day, they were "opening up" new states, they moved the Supreme Palace to a whole floor in the Commerce Building, Jones started a weekly paper, *The Cyclops,* and he hired three more men in the crypt of propagation.

It was about then I woke up to two things, the changing type of "literature" we were putting out and the source of the majority of new memberships. The literature, which had been "patriotic" and "benevolent" and "fraternal" and wouldn't have stirred the passions or prejudices of a child, began deliberately to bait the Catholics and Jews. And in one week, Jones bragged, he got more members from Indiana alone than the entire Jungle of the Southeast.

But before going into the causes behind that, let's take a look at the only woman officer of the Red Riders, the Supreme Pythoness, Mrs. Rosebud Boggs.

CHAPTER THREE

HAD BEEN WORKING TWO WEEKS FOR THE RED Riders before I
saw Mrs. Boggs. On my first day I noticed on one of the Doc's
proclamations, "Approved, R. B.," and I learned that all my copy
must be approved by "R. B." and that I couldn't get a new pencil
or a fresh typewriter ribbon unless "R. B." okayed the requisition
on the crypt of supplies.

"You'll have to get an 'R. B.' on that," said one of the typists
in the crypt of propagation.

She was a flashy brunette, dumb as they come but with a
swell pair of legs. All the girls around the shop had good legs.
Whoever hired them must have operated on the theory that the
Red Riders might need a chorus some day. I guess it was Jones.

"Who is this R. B.?" I asked her.

"That's Mrs. Boggs, Supreme Pythoness. There don't nothing
move around here without she says so. Specially money."

The name didn't mean anything to me—that night on Fern
Street I didn't know whose apartment we were in—and when I
finally saw "R. B.," I didn't recognize her at first.

She sent for me. I came into a big private office where the
Supreme Pythoness sat at a desk like a railroad president's.
You'd never have known her for the fat blonde who cried all over
George X. Jones. This woman was a red-head and, while she was
fat, she had it covered up with a coat-suit and swell furs—a funny
thing to wear at work—and I reckon a corset that gave her a front
as impressive as a pouter pigeon's. She had on glasses, too, that

made her look severe, one of those dinky rimless pairs on a gold chain.

"Mr. Dudley," she said, "I want your advice and suggestions. We are organizing a ladies' auxiliary of the O-R-R and we must have a good name. What do you think of this one?"

She handed over a slip of paper. On it was printed "Sisters of the Scarlet Circle."

I said, "I don't think much of it."

"Why not?"

"Well"—and I looked straight at her—"it makes you think of scarlet women."

She blushed—yes, sir, she blushed as pinky as a girl and all the powder on her went funny and fuzzy.

"I'm afraid you're right," she said. "The thought wouldn't have entered my head, but of course so many people are evil-minded."

I didn't say thank you.

"What else would you propose?" she said.

I said why not change it to Sisters of the Silver Circle or some other color or even Sisters of the Red Circle. Mrs. Boggs said she would think it over and, sure enough, they did call it Sisters of the Red Circle and I guess nobody was evil-minded about that because it eventually became a big thing and a lot of respectable women joined it.

"Thank you for your help," she told me and she gave me a nice smile. "Perhaps I shall call on you later for some more of your rear actions."

I looked at her hard but it was plain she didn't mean to be funny. It took me sometime to learn that Mrs. Boggs had a fondness for fancy words but frequently got them balled up.

"Thank you, ma'am," I said. And it was just that minute that something flashed over me. I'd been puzzling my head over having seen this woman before somewhere and when I turned and faced the door, I knew where. Over the door was a picture, "The Death of Little Nell."

I went back to my desk thinking, Well, sir, so that's who "R. B." is, George X. Jones' girl, and he made her Supreme Pythoness!

It didn't occur to me then that she might have done more for Jones than he did for her.

Mrs. Boggs was a pretty good egg. She kept an eagle eye on the finances around the place and she'd fire a stenographer like that if she caught her cheating the time-clock or running up telephone calls to a sweetie. But she didn't care if the girls sneaked a cigarette or if she caught one necking with a King Cobra in the back hall.

She was good at her job, too, I guess. Whoever the treasurer was in the individual Lairs, the treasurer of the Supreme Palace was the Pythoness. She ran the books and received all the collection mail and the King Cobras reported first to her when they came to town. She was a mighty ignorant woman in many ways, but she knew her arithmetic.

Another thing she was good at was keeping Doc Sloat decent. Outwardly, he'd undergone a remarkable transformation from the old ragbag and town drunkard of a few months before. He still toted his "sword cane," but his "linen," sir, was clean every day or at least every other day, his pants were pressed, his shoes were shined, he'd bought a cutaway coat and a flock of fancy vests and Mrs. Boggs made him go to the barbershop every morning.

She stood over him and kept after him like a hen with a chick. He had a little habit, when he was in the grand crypt, of taking off his shoes and sitting in his sock feet, and one day Mrs. Boggs caught him at it. I was in there with him, going over a proclamation, and heard the bawling-out she gave him.

"Why, Doctor, what do you mean slopping around here practically barefooted? Suppose some of the Terrible Tarantulas came in from Indiana or Pennsylvania or some of those northern states. And you the Supreme Serpent! What would they think? It ain't dignified," she said, "and it ain't nice."

"They hurt me," said the Doc, watering at the eyes.

"Your feet? Then you ought to do something about 'em. I'll tell you what, I'll send you to my chiropractor."

She meant her chiropodist and she did send him to a chiropodist and I don't know how well he fixed the Doc's feet, but he wore shoes after that, even in the grand crypt.

"A sterling soul," he called Mrs. Boggs. "The queen of her sex! It is women like Mrs. Boggs who made America great. Molly Pitcher, Betsy Ross, Martha Washington—or was it Mary?—anyhow, George's mother. Motherhood, womanhood, purity, sanctity—they are the warp and woof of our Order."

I believe he really admired Mrs. Boggs and liked being bossed by her.

She tried to stop his drinking, too, but she was a total failure there, for nothing pleased her better than a little nip herself. When five o'clock came and the Supreme Palace officially closed and most of the help left, she usually found an excuse to be in the Doc's office, where she stalled around until he brought out the bottle.

She always pretended to be shocked. "Oh, Doctor—again? You promised me! What is it, still that dreadful corn?"

"My first today, ma'am," he would assure her, already so drunk he couldn't stand up. "Physician's orders—must taper off gradually—why not join me in a small libation? It will do you good, Mrs. Boggs."

"Oh, I couldn't think of it—and that awful corn!—well, just one if you insist"—and by that time Mrs. Boggs would have her nose in the glass, taking it neat where strong men would have fainted.

These little sessions generally wound up with Mrs. Boggs tipsy and swearing the Doc on the water wagon.

She got weepy or she got mean when she'd had too many. I used to stick around to accept the Doc's hospitality and, believe me, the change from Mrs. Boggs' office manner was startling. Where she was all business, she became sentimental, where she had been shrewd and cold, she got maudlin or tough and she forgot all about using those big words. She used some mighty short ones and there was no doubt about what they meant.

"That Lila Lee," she would say, "is a sweet petty, just a sweet petty," for she was a great movie fan and would fight for her favorite stars like a she-bear for her young. "But that other bitch"—a leading vampire of the day—"makes me sick to my stomach," and she would be off on a tirade that left no doubt Mrs. Boggs was pure in heart.

Her other preoccupations, besides children and romantic love, were death and animals. She turned first to the mortuary notices in the daily paper to see if any of her friends had died, she loved nothing better than a good funeral and her career had apparently teemed with pets. They ranged from horses to canary birds. All of them had died, however, and Mrs. Boggs had given them funerals and wept over their graves.

"Henery," she said to me, "nobody ever loved me like that dog did—I'll never forget poor Henery!" and tears just oozed out of her.

I asked George X. Jones about this habit of hers of calling everything and everybody "Henery" when she was in her cups, and he said she had a son once named Henry who died or ran away or something. She didn't like to talk about it, George said, but the name was on her mind and it was always easy to catch her on the soft side by calling her "mamma."

"But that's my candy, son," he grinned. "Don't burn your fingers."

"You're welcome to it, Henery," I told him.

He was a shameless rascal. He didn't like their drinking, but I think he deliberately encouraged it, to hit Mrs. Boggs for dough, I suppose, and to keep the Doc from messing around too much in the finances and politics of the Order. So long as Sloat was plastered most of the time and Mrs. Boggs could be softened up when he needed a touch, George X. Jones could run things pretty much his own way.

You may say that I haven't much room to talk when I was working for them and taking their pay and hobnobbing with them, and you may be right. This isn't my story and I'm not making apologies. I did a lot of things when I was younger that I might not do today, that extra thirty dollars was a godsend to a forty-dollar-a-week reporter and I'll admit I liked hanging around the Palace, where the atmosphere was free and easy and the girls friendly. After all, at that time the Order of Red Riders seemed harmless, if silly, and what was good enough for the *New York Sphere* was good enough for me. So when Mrs. Boggs invited me to go with them on a week-end jaunt in the country, I said sure and got a day off from the paper.

It seems that in Bellweather County the local Red Riders were going to hold a Reptilon. It seems Mrs. Boggs, though she was Supreme Pythoness, had never seen one. And it seems that Bellweather County was where she was born. She hadn't been back there for years and years and this would be a swell chance not only to attend a Reptilon but to see the house she was born in and look up old friends and find out what had happened to them and who had died.

"Why, my folks owned slaves there before the Civil War," she said. "Some of those old niggers are still alive. I remember when

I was a kiddie my old black mammy used to hold me on her lap and tell me stories about Br'er Rabbit and Br'er Fox and sing me songs like 'Swing Low, Sweet Chariot.' She used to take me fishing, too. We used to catch catfish and fry 'em on the creek bank and they were the best thing I ever tasted. Lord, Lord! how I'd love to sink my teeth in a good hot cat again!"

The followup on this was that Mrs. Boggs began to plan a fish fry. We would drive down to Bell-weather County Saturday morning, have the fish fry Saturday afternoon, see the Reptilon Saturday night, stay at the hotel in Mirchison, the county-seat, and drive back Sunday. She wrote a friend of hers in Mirchison and he wrote back and said it was all arranged and, when Saturday came, here we went, five of us in Mrs. Boggs' big Cadillac.

There was Jones driving, and a Miss Kitty Cooper in the front seat with him, and Mrs. Boggs and a friend of hers named Mr. Vasco in the back with me. Doc Sloat said he was going but he couldn't get up in time. Nobody minded leaving him behind.

Miss Cooper was supposed to be my girl for the day. She was a cute little trick, not much more than five feet, with a pair of big black eyes and the prettiest legs I ever saw. She didn't mind flashing all she had, either. I'd met her only a few days before, when she came to work in the auditing crypt, and it never would have occurred to me to invite her. Jones did that. He told Mrs. Boggs I wanted her and he asked me to play ball. That was all right with me. But I could see from the minute she hopped in the front seat with Jones that I wasn't going to make much time with Kitty.

Mrs. Boggs teased me about my new flame and Kitty laughed and I didn't let on. The Supreme Pythoness was feeling mighty amiable and she was too excited about going back to the old home town to notice if Jones was putting anything over on her or not. Besides, Mr. Vasco claimed her attention. He was a queer one.

A dark, squatty fellow, with a big bush of hair and blue gills like he needed a shave, he was evidently some sort of foreigner. A Spaniard, I thought, judging by his name, but he said no, he was not one of those damn Spaniard, he was not one of those damn Italian, either, he was a Corsican and a direct descendant of Napoleon Bonaparte. He looked to me like one of those damn liar.

I couldn't figure how he came in on the party. Jones was introduced to him at the same time I was, when we called for him at the Metropole, a small hotel with not too good a reputation, and Miss Cooper was introduced to him when we went by for her. Mrs. Boggs called him "Mr." Vasco, so she couldn't have known him long. But she made a big fuss over him, asking if he was comfortable and how he liked the South and pointing out cotton fields and things like that.

Mr. Vasco was an out-of-towner and, if his English was any indication, not long in the country, either. I thought he was a visiting Cobra or Tarantula, but it turned out he didn't know anything about the Red Riders. He was going to "fry the feesh," that's all he knew, and when I mentioned the Reptilon, he didn't know what I meant. I began to explain, but Jones turned around and said something to shut me up. Evidently the Imperial Python and the Supreme Pythoness were traveling incognito. "Those Red Rider, he is like the banditti, yes?" said Vasco, and I let it go at that.

Bellweather County is more than a hundred miles from Vesta, in one of the prettiest parts of the state, I think. You come down from the hills into rolling valleys where the red creeks run through some of the richest farmland in the world. They've learned to diversify their crops here. The earth is green with alfalfa, tobacco grows, and peanuts and pecans, and a little later you come into miles and miles of peach orchards. Spring breaks early in our state. By March the peach trees are blooming and where there is cotton, the fields are pink and white and that pale green color. Then the canebrakes begin to thicken along the bottoms, the towns and cabins get further apart and pretty soon you're in Bellweather, the heart of the plantation country.

We bowled along over good roads under a cloudless sky and it was pretty swell. About eleven o'clock Mrs. Boggs said we must stop for a snack and she hauled out a hamper of fried chicken and a gallon jug of corn liquor. Jones didn't want to stop, he said we must make Mirchison by noon and, anyway, it was foolishness to eat now when we were going to a fish fry. But Mrs. Boggs made him.

We pulled up where there was a well alongside the road and a woman came down from a house with buttermilk which she wouldn't let us pay for. Jones drank buttermilk and the rest of us had a shot of corn. Mr. Vasco never had tasted corn before. He laughed when we told him it was strong. In his country, he said, they had the strongest brandy in the world and he used to drink a glass of it every morning before breakfast. But I noticed he shuddered when Mrs. Boggs' stuff went down. It was good corn, too, aged and yellow, and tasted fine with cold well-water out of a gourd. Miss Cooper took hers straight without a blink and Mrs. Boggs had another shot before we drove on. Nobody ate any chicken.

Two years before, when I was working in Margana, I'd been to Mirchison on the so-called "convict king" investigation. The "convict king" was old Asa Tucker, a big planter and a power in that section. When the state used to hire out convict labor to private individuals, he had a thousand niggers working for him and after the legislature stopped the system, he kept right on working niggers like slaves.

"But how like slave?" said Vasco, when I was telling them about it. "The state say 'no'—how he get Negro without the state give permish?"

"Oh, he got 'em legally enough after a fashion. Down here, when a white man wants a nigger, he pays him out of the chaingang. Then the nigger has to work out his debt to the white man. Of course, he never does. The white man charges him for his board and keep and maybe lets him have a dollar once in a while and the nigger never does catch up with what he owes. It's peonage, but in most counties the officials wink at it."

Vasco couldn't understand.

"If I those Negro, I run away."

"That's what some of Tucker's niggers did. He caught 'em and whipped 'em and the next time they ran away, he whipped them so hard he killed a couple. He chained the bodies in Chalk Creek, in the rapids where they would rot. But before they rotted good, the Sheriff found them and he couldn't overlook two dead men, even niggers. That's when they got after Tucker."

"They leench him, yes?"

"Certainly not!—but they did send him to jail for ten years, him and his two sons, and the nigger overseer who did the actual whipping got life. You can't get a white jury to convict a white man of a nigger's murder in this state."

Vasco pondered.

"If I Negro here, I keel white man before he keel me," he said very positively.

I looked at Mrs. Boggs and she looked at Vasco kind of disturbed.

"You mustn't talk like that," she said, "or you'll get into trouble. This is a white man's country and we have to keep the niggers down. They've been restless since that Asa Tucker business. That's why—"

She shut up, but I knew she was thinking about the Reptilon.

"Just the same," said Vasco, "I keel him good. Any man—white—black—wheep me, I cut him out by the heart."

After a minute I said, "Oh, it's not as bad as all that. Most of the white people treat their niggers pretty well. They stand for a lot, too, more shiftlessness and worthlessness than any employer in the world stands for. And the niggers like the system. You take the average nigger and he'd rather steal than work and he'd rather live off a white man's generosity than do either. When a white man pays a nigger out of jail, he doesn't need him half the time. Maybe he wants a patch of land plowed and that's all. But by the time it's plowed, that nigger is his nigger. He'll have a shack on the white man's place, he'll be wearing the white man's old clothes, he'll be eating what the white man's cook gives him—and she'll give him plenty—and the white man will be recognizing a sort of obligation to keep on taking care of that nigger. He'll think to himself, 'Oh, well, he's a handy nigger to have around,' and if the nigger never does anotner lick of work, he'll be that white man's nigger till he dies. Ain't that so, Mrs. Boggs?"

"It certainly is!" she said.

Vasco didn't say anything for a minute. Then he said, "Just those same, I keel him."

How can you argue with a guy like that? I shut up. But I decided right there that I didn't want any part of Mr. Vasco.

Mrs. Boggs began talking about the niggers that used to work for her folks. She said they were the laziest but the sweetest niggers that ever lived and she bet if she saw them again they would recognize her and call her "Miss Rosy" and pet her like they did when she was a child. Soon after that we got to Mirchison and found Mrs. Boggs' friend at the hotel and drove out a piece in the country, and sure enough, when we stopped in front of this log cabin, a pair of the oldest and blackest niggers you ever saw ran out yelling, "It's Miss Rosy, Miss Rosy!" and Mrs. Boggs broke down and cried and we were all mighty affected.

But it looked to me, till Mrs. Boggs piled out of the car, as if the niggers were making a dead set for Miss Cooper and when Mrs. Boggs' friend, a Dr. Parker, gave me a wink over his shoulder, I would have laid a little bet that Miss Rosy and the old family retainers never had set eyes on each other before.

The cabin stood in a grove of pines on a bluff above Chalk Creek and it was one of the cleanest, neatest places you ever set foot in. There was a little organ in the parlor and a Bible on the table, rag rugs on the floor and around the room at least six easels, supporting those big, hand-colored portraits you find mostly in the country, where itinerant photographers tramp around and sell them to the farmers and the colored people. All of these portraits were of colored people, dressed in their Sunday best and mighty dignified-looking.

"Who is that, auntie?" Miss Cooper said to the old woman.

"Why, law, chile, dat's me!"

Miss Cooper giggled. I wished she hadn't. The old woman had on a turban and a calico dress, she was black as the ace of spades, and the portrait was of a light-complexioned young woman with frizzlety hair and a lace fichu around her neck. You couldn't much blame Miss Cooper for not recognizing it; but I wish she hadn't laughed just the same.

We went into the bedroom and the kitchen and that house was spotless all the way through. Every chair had a tidy on its back, and the kindling was bound with bright ribbons, the bedroom smelled of lavender and the kitchen of spices and savory cooking. The old woman apologized for the cooking smell. She was stewing a mess of dewberries for Uncle Nitch's sweet tooth, she said, but if we'd be so kind as to rest ourselves on the front porch, where it was nice and shady, she'd get busy on the fish.

We sat down in split-bottomed chairs with the tidies on them, the breeze came sighing and soughing through the pines, we looked at the sunshine on the tops of young corn and it was hard to believe that down there, beyond the rail fence, was Asa Tucker's land and on clear nights you might have heard from here the clanking of the chains where the bodies swung in the rapids.

"Did you ever hear them, uncle?" I asked the old man.

"Who—me? I ain't heard nothin' and I ain't seed nothin' and I don't know nothin' a-tall."

Dr. Parker laughed.

"You won't get any niggers around here to talk about that business. Not since the Red Riders begun to operate. They say they called the other night on a nigger other side of Muscadine who'd been shootin' off his mouth too free. They just went in and looked at him and drunk about a gallon of water out of his bucket and said, 'Nigger, hump yourself,' and he lit out for the county line and I reckon he's runnin' yet."

I looked at Mrs. Boggs and Jones, but they both sat there quiet as the cat that swallowed the cream. Mr. Vasco, who'd cooled down considerably since we reached the cabin, opened his mouth to say something, but Mrs. Boggs kicked him in the foot and he shut up.

"I think the Red Riders are wonderful, don't you?" said Miss Cooper, winking at Jones.

"Oh, I reckon they're all right," Parker said. "Some folks around here seem to think it's a bad thing and ought to be broke up, but I reckon they do a lot of good in a way." He laughed kind of self-consciously. "They ain't asked me to join yet. If they do, reckon I'll have to buy me a red blanket and a horse just to keep on the safe side!"

"By the way, Miss Rosy," he said to Mrs. Boggs, "they're fixing to burn one of their serpents tonight out on the Mill Creek Road. Maybe youall would like to see it."

"How cute!" said Miss Cooper. "Can anybody go?"

"Sure, and I guess everybody will but the niggers," said Parker, and we all said we wanted to go and he started talking to Mrs. Boggs about people she used to know in the county and who was dead and who wasn't.

He seemed like a right nice little fellow but young and simple for a doctor. Later on it turned out he wasn't a real doctor, but just worked in the drugstore, which his uncle owned. He let that out while he was showing me around the cabin and telling me about the old niggers.

"See that center-beam? It's a hundred and forty years old. The first Moody to settle hereabouts cut it with his own hands when he built this house. The Moodys are the biggest folks in the county now, but they lived here for years and when they finally built that big place you saw where we turned off the main road, old Mr. Andrew Moody give this cabin to Uncle Nitch and Aunt Decia. They're good niggers and I reckon they're near as old as the cabin. They get it rent free and make their livin' out of fish fries. Everybody comes out here when they want to hold a fry."

"I thought Uncle Nitch and Aunt Decia used to work for Mrs. Boggs' folks," I said.

He winked at me. "Shucks, I put 'em up to that. When I fixed it for the fry, I said, 'It's for Miss Rosy; you remember Miss Rosy, don't you?' and they said sure they did. You can't get niggers like that to say they don't remember nobody."

I said, "You've known Mrs. Boggs a long time, haven't you?"

He didn't say anything for a minute and then he said, "Pretty long—come on, let's go back out," and we went.

The rest of the crowd was having a mint julep made out of corn, and we had one, too, and after that we all had another and then Aunt Decia set a long pine table under the trees and we sat down and ate. We had catfish fried and catfish stew. We had ham fried and cold ham and hot ham gravy. We had roasted yams and turnip greens and string beans cooked with salt pork. We had hot biscuits and corn pones baked in ashes. We had green tomato pickles and pickled watermelon rind and pickled peaches. We had all kinds of jellies and preserves. When we were about to founder, Aunt Decia came out with three big dewberry pies, so I guess Uncle Nitch didn't get that mess for his sweet tooth, after all.

Everybody had been pretty noisy when we first sat down. Mrs. Boggs was sounding off about her childhood and acting mighty kittenish. She started calling Mr. Vasco "Henery" and feeding him titbits like he was a kid, and he would crack those blue jaws full of fish and laugh to beat the band. "You are my sweet mam-ma!" he said, and I could see by George X. Jones' eyes that he didn't like that a bit. But even he was getting his fun, laughing and panting and coming back for more when Miss Cooper would pretend to slap him and tell him to keep his hands above the table. She was the life of the party, cutting those black eyes at everybody and getting young Dr. Parker in a regular sweat. I thought he was going to choke once or twice, trying to eat and look both. But by the time we finished the pies, things quieted down.

Mrs. Boggs yawned and said if she didn't get forty winks she'd never make the Reptilon.

Miss Cooper said she felt sleepy, too.

Aunt Decia, who was clearing the table, said maybe the ladies would like to lie down a spell and Mrs. Boggs said she would.

Jones spoke up quick to Miss Cooper—"What you need is a little walk," he said—and after Mrs. Boggs went in the cabin, those two took the path toward the creek.

That left me and Dr. Parker and Vasco.

I took one look at them and said I needed a nap mighty bad. I found one in a hammock Uncle Nitch slung between two pines.

It was almost dark when I woke up. Voices woke me and I lay there a minute and listened. Vasco and Parker were on the front porch, arguing the nigger question. I heard Vasco say, "I keel those man if I Negro!" and I got up and walked over to where they sat with the jug between them.

"You better go slow on that stuff, mister," I said to Vasco. "That's mighty strong stuff."

"Aw, he's all right, he's a foreigner and don't know enough to talk better," said Parker. I hadn't meant the talk, but I let it go at that.

If Parker was drunk, you couldn't tell it except by his eyes, which looked like fried eggs. Vasco was so drunk he didn't know who I was.

He began to curse me, calling me a nigger-killer, and before we knew it he was struggling to his feet and trying to open a knife. I could have slapped him down with one finger—a baby could have—but somebody knocked the knife out of his hand. It was Mrs. Boggs. She'd come out from the cabin without our seeing her.

"You big fool!" she yelled.

Vasco fell back on his bottom and goggled at her. If he recognized her, I guess the change in his "mam-ma" knocked him speechless.

"Gimme that thing!" she yelled, and Vasco picked up the knife without a word and handed it to her. She whirled around.

"Where's the rest of 'em? Where's George?"

"I reckon they went for a little stroll, Miss Rosy," said Parker.

"Don't you 'Miss Rosy' me. I'm sick of it!" she snapped. "Go find him! We're going to this what-chucall it, ain't we? Well, for God's sake let's get goin'!" I guess she'd sobered up just enough for her liquor to turn mean on her.

I'd been standing stockstill, hot one minute and cold the next, for nobody had ever pulled a knife on me before, but suddenly I knew I had to get away from there quick.

"I'll find them," I said.

After I'd put my lunch at the bottom of the hill, I found them.

"We were just coming along," said Jones, looking smug.

"Has Miss Rosy woke up yet?" said Miss Cooper, smiling brightly.

"She has," I said, "and you better not call her 'Miss Rosy.' And you better brush those pine needles off both of you before she sees you."

We all drove along to the Reptilon without much conversation, but I rode in the front seat with Jones and Miss Cooper. I didn't feel so good, either, thinking about that wop behind me, not even when Miss Cooper tickled my hand in the dark. She was certainly big-hearted, that girl.

CHAPTER FOUR

WE CUT BACK THROUGH MIRCHISON TO REACH the Mill Creek Road. It's a little town but an old one and to my notion there's nothing nicer than a little old southern town at twilight on a spring evening. Honeysuckle in the fence corners, fireflies in the courthouse square, locusts and tree-frogs beginning to sing and lights shining from the windows across the deep lawns and the people on their porches. Pretty soon the young girls come strolling by in their white dresses to meet their sweethearts down at the drug-store, and it's dark and soft and warm and the friendliest-seeming place on earth. Mirchison is that kind of town. But there were precious few people either on the porches or in the square when we went through, and not a nigger in hearing. When we had passed the hotel and the jail and the railroad station, we found out why. Every automobile in Mirchison must have been on that Mill Creek Road, all heading in the same direction.

We turned on our lights and honked the horn and managed to squeeze by some of them, but when we got to where we were going, we had trouble finding space to park. Jones finally twisted in between a Ford and a big Hudson on a high bank above what looked like a cow pasture. Down there it was so black you couldn't see anything but dim lines of fence on one side, woods on the other and what appeared to be a flagpole sticking up at the far end of the pasture where it sloped over the rise. But up where we were it was brighter, the headlights of a hundred cars crisscrossed back and forth and you could see plenty.

Half the white population of the county must have been there. People were sitting easy in their cars, people were swarming up to get places at the edge of the bank and people were visiting around from car to car like this was a picnic or a sociable. The women were there, and the children, and most of them were pretty nice-looking folks. I judged we were among the first families of Mirchison and that they'd come out here like they would to a minstrel show or a circus.

In the Hudson next to us were three fellows and four girls. Two of the girls were teasing the man at the wheel, a big, upstanding fellow who looked like he'd played college football once and could still take out a tackle if he wanted to. He was trying to be good-natured, but you could see the kidding was getting his goat. Nobody was having much to say in our car and we heard every word next door.

"My goodness, Penny, I never expected you up here tonight," one of the girls was saying. "Why aren't you out there with your friends? Lost your red flannels?"

"Wore 'em out ridin' 'round, Betty Sue."

"Why, hon, I would've made you some more. Why didn't you let me know? I'd just love to help you boys haunt somebody."

"That's not why he's renegin'," the other girl said. "He couldn't find a horse!"

"You won't see many horses out there tonight," one of the other men cut in. "More likely mules."

"Penny can ride a mule," the first girl said. "Bet he'd look cute as a bug in a red nightgown on a mule. Which are you, Penny, one of those cobras or a little old garter snake?"

The rest laughed and the big guy didn't say anything, but when Betty Sue started in on him again, he spoke up.

"Cut it out, will you? You know how I feel about those damn skunks. My father helped start the old Red Riders. He'd turn in his grave if he knew who was in them now. I don't think this is funny."

There was a little silence at that and I heard Parker in the back of our car whisper, "It's Pendleton Moody—you remember him, Miss Rosy." They must have heard Parker in the Hudson, too, for they all turned and looked. One of the men said, "Hi, Doc," and the girls smiled kind of faintly. None of them spoke to Mrs. Boggs, but it was getting darker all the time and our top was up. Maybe they didn't recognize her.

Then nobody had a chance to talk. Away off somewhere, a bugle blew. It blew once, loud and high, and when the sound died, you couldn't hear a breath. About the same minute, where the flagpole sat, came a little spurt of fire and the next thing a running flame. It ran right up the pole and branched off to both sides at the top, and there it kept burning, wriggling and rippling in the night. I don't know how they did it—mostly with kerosene and rope, I guess—but it did look like a live golden snake and a whopping big one, too.

"Here they come!" somebody in the crowd hollered, and sure enough, over the rise and riding hell-bent for election, charged a thing on a horse. I call it a "thing" because that's what it was, all bunched and floppy and blood-red under the torch and the next second black against the glare as it headed full-tilt down the slope. You couldn't make out the cobra specs till it was close, but if I'd been a nigger I wouldn't have waited that long.

Whoever he was, that Red Rider could ride. He stopped his horse all in a heap, r'ared him back on his hindlegs and lifted his right arm. He didn't make a sound while he held the pose and the horse pawed the air. I tell you it was pretty fine—Buffalo Bill couldn't have done it better.

In a minute he wheeled and trotted back halfway. Then he stopped and in another minute the rest of the Red Riders came over the rise. The fellow in the Hudson was right—they weren't riding, not even mules; they were marching two abreast and there were only forty or fifty of them. But when they spread out across the pasture in a semi-circle, with the black woods behind them and the serpent burning in the black sky, they looked like a hundred and they were woeful, wild, weird and every other word in Doc Sloat's booger-bag. They all had on the cobra hoods and robes, you understand, and nothing to tell them apart except one man, who carried the American flag.

The flag-bearer walked out from the rest and stood beside the man on the horse and a third man stepped out beside him. He lifted both arms in some sort of sign and he spoke in a voice you could have heard a mile.

"What?" said one of the girls in the Hudson. "What did he say?"

Not more than three people in the crowd could have told her. I was one of them, but I didn't. What he said was, "Cum clab ad Clastra!"

Up to then I'd been as spellbound as anybody else, but I had to let go a snicker at that. And when he started his speech, I snickered some more, for it was the same old eyewash about liberty, fraternity and sacred womanhood, and most of it I'd written myself.

I listened with half an ear to the speaker and half an ear to the remarks in the Hudson, which weren't complimentary. Most of them came from the fellow at the wheel. If Buck Somebody thought he could get elected on that sort of bunk, he was saying, he didn't know much about the people of Bellweather County, and he went on to give the whole bunch in the pasture hell.

Pretty soon I began to catch another voice. It was in our car and it was Mrs. Boggs'.

"Is that so?" she would mumble, "is that so? All right, if you don't like it, you know what you can do—if you don't like it, you can lump it!" and Parker would try to hush her up and she would trail off into more mumbles of which "bastard" and "son-of-a-bitch" was about all you could understand.

I thought at first she was talking about the speaker and I said to myself, my God, the old lady is drunk sure enough, knocking her own crowd. But then I got it—she was sore at the guy in the Hudson.

By and by the speaker really warmed up.

"I say to you," he boomed, "that Anglo-Saxon blood has always dominated and always will! It fed Alfred when he wrote the charter of English liberty; it gathered about Hampden as he stood beneath the oak; it thundered in Cromwell's veins as he fought his king; it humbled Napoleon at Waterloo; it has touched the desert and the jungle with undying glory; it carried the drumbeat of England around the world and spread on every continent the gospel of liberty and of God; it established this Republic, carved it from wilderness, conquered it from the Indians, wrested it from England and at last, stilling its own tumult, consecrated it forever as the home of the Anglo-Saxon and the theater of his transcending achievement. Never one foot of it can be surrendered, while that blood lives in American veins and feeds American hearts, to the domination of an alien and inferior race!"

From the audience in the pasture went up a yell, and some people on the bank clapped and cheered.

"What a damn shame!" I heard the fellow in the Hudson say. "He stole that outright from Henry Grady's speeches. I used to recite it in school. Next thing he'll be giving us Spartacus to the gladiators."

I blushed, remembering where I'd lifted that stuff. But I didn't have much chance to feel remorseful. Mrs. Boggs stuck her head from the side of our car and cut loose.

"Who you calling a thief, Pen Moody? You and your dirty family that stole the food out of honest folks' mouths and ain't fitten to breathe the same air with 'em!"

She had her dander up. I guess she'd been hitting the bottle on the quiet, too.

"You big bunch of nothin' you!" she screamed.

Jones twisted around in the front seat and jammed his hand in her face, Parker grabbed her arms and she flopped back, squirming and spitting. People were standing up in their cars, looking our way, and somebody cut a flashlight. But it was too dark to see much.

We got her quiet after a minute. She began to snuffle and Parker was petting her, I guess. I could hear him say, "There, there, Miss Rosy—don't you mind—there, there!" Vasco must have been asleep or scared stiff, for we didn't hear a peep from him. Miss Cooper just giggled and felt around for my hand. I gave it to her. Jones said, "I'm going to get out of this."

I don't know what the people in the Hudson were doing. They hadn't spoken a word since Mrs. Boggs blew up, but just as Jones got the Cadillac backed and turned, a voice hollered, "Taking your friends home, Doc?" I was surprised when Parker yelled, "What's it to you, big mouth?" I didn't think he had the guts.

We didn't leave too soon. While we were backing, that fellow ended his speech and it was all over. Up on the bank, other cars started their engines and down in the pasture the Red Riders were re-forming and marching away with the man on horseback at their head. The burning serpent had gone out and was just a prickle of coals in the dark, but the moon was up and when I looked back, I saw the last of the Riders disappearing over the rise like a file of ghosts returning to the graveyard.

At the hotel, there was a row.

Everybody had separate rooms, but we all clumped up to Mrs. Boggs' who had the biggest. We must have been a sad-looking outfit—Jones humped over a chairback, chewing his nails; Vasco propped against the wall, glum and blinking and his jaws bluer than ever; Parker, his countryman's face like greasy bacon, fussing with the window as if he was host and had to make everybody at home; Mrs. Boggs spread out in the middle of the bed with her hair stringy and her cheeks, where she'd cried, like a barn door when the paint's run; and me and Miss Cooper bringing up the rear, in no mood for cheers on my part, anyway.

Miss Cooper went to the bathroom and I parked on the only other chair.

"Make me a drink, hon, I'm dead beat," Mrs. Boggs said to Parker, who'd brought up the jug.

He looked at it and there was only about a quarter of an inch washing around the bottom.

"Ain't enough for a round," he said.

"Then go fetch some more—get another gallon—they used to make some mighty tolerable corn in Bellweather County."

At that, Jones got up. He popped his fingers like a man shooting crap.

"Look here, all you hogs—I won't stand for it—you've already drunk a gallon on this trip and you ain't a-going to drink any more!—if you do, I won't be responsible."

We all looked at him. Parker was halfway to the door. Vasco glowered from the wall. I guess I wasn't so cordial myself. I needed a drink.

"All right, Miss Buttermilk, who cares what you'll be responsible for?" said Mrs. Boggs. "Who cares about you, anyhow?"

"But look here, Rosy, you're drunk."

"You're mighty right I'm drunk, and I'm gonna be drunker. Go get the gallon, hon."

Jones appealed to Parker.

"Listen, fellow, she mustn't have any more. We got things to do. We got important people to see."

"You see 'em," said Mrs. Boggs. "I want a drink right now."

"Well, just one," said Jones.

But when she had the drink in her hand, she sat up in bed and glared at him.

"You're the son-of-a-bitch hit me this afternoon," she said, and threw the glass in his face.

Jones stood for a second with the corn liquor dripping off him like sweat. Then he walked over and popped her with his palm.

"That'll teach you!"

None of us moved except Mrs. Boggs, who pitched over and bawled. Speaking for myself, I believe in southern chivalry, but I wouldn't have cared much if he'd knocked her cold. I was fed up.

"That'll teach her!" Jones bragged to the rest of us.

Then Vasco let out a kind of hoot and went right across the bed and Mrs. Boggs on it.

When Parker and I got to them, Vasco had Jones against the wall, choking him. I don't know what makes men think they've always got to stop a fight if they know the fighters, but it's a good thing for Jones we felt that way.

While we held Vasco, Jones got up, both hands to his neck.

"I'm gonna be sick," he said, and he was.

After that, things were pretty messy for a while. Miss Cooper had come out of the bathroom and was trying to calm Mrs. Boggs, and she thought Vasco had hit Mrs. Boggs and started calling him a brute, and he couldn't make her understand any different, and it looked for a little like there was going to be another brawl right there. While they were jawing and jabbering at each other, Parker got a towel and I helped him clean up the floor, and then we got another towel for Miss Rosy's face, and a drink for her, and by the time the dust was settled, Jones had gone and there was no more liquor in the jug.

I looked at Mrs. Boggs sitting in the middle of the bed crying into her glass, I looked at Miss Cooper on one side of her and Vasco on the other, and I looked at Parker and I said, "You and me might as well fetch that gallon."

We got it at a place down the street back of the jail and I got a pint for myself.

"You take it on back to them," I said. "I've got to give a Chinaman a banjo lesson."

"Sho' 'nough?" said Parker. He wasn't the brightest boy in school.

I trailed him to the hotel, where I went to my room and had a bath and changed my shirt and made me a long drink with ice and lemon and sugar. It was good corn, but it wasn't as good as Mrs. Boggs'. Then I slipped out the back way and took a walk.

It was nice in that little town, with the moon shining through the shade trees and some streets so quiet you'd have thought it was 'way late and in others just the soft talk of people you couldn't see in the dark. In one house they were giving a dance and I watched for a while from across the street, the couples weaving past the windows and music from a nigger band instead of a victrola and every now and then a couple coming out and strolling up and down or maybe sitting in one of the automobiles in front. The man would light a cigarette and generally the girl would, too, and you could hear them sweet-talking each other without understanding the words, and pretty soon the sparks would go out and you couldn't hear anything and you didn't wonder an awful lot whether he was kissing her or not. Some niggers came along and watched with me for a while, and though they laughed and pranked with each other, they didn't make any cracks, and when they went away, laughing and nudging along the street, I felt like they were good niggers and they must have pretty good times in this town, too.

I didn't feel like going back to the hotel or seeing anybody in my crowd, but after I'd stopped at the greasy spoon across from the railroad station and had me some ham and eggs, I went on back and, sure enough, there was Parker in the lobby and I went over and asked him how things were.

It seemed right away that things weren't so good and it didn't take a detective to figure that they were worse than that with Parker. He was just about two-thirds drunker than I'd thought he could ever get. But, Lordy, how he could talk.

We sat down in the lobby, with nobody near but the night clerk, who was half asleep, and Parker talked to me for two hours. He told me everything that had happened and he told me a lot more.

He said when he got back to the hotel, he took the gallon upstairs and he and Miss Rosy and Vasco and Miss Cooper had drinks. Vasco and Miss Cooper had made it up, Miss Rosy was feeling better and everything was fine. They sent Parker to look for me and they even tried to find Jones, for Miss Rosy, it seems, was all for forgiving Jones and told Vasco he must forgive him, too, and apologize to Jones and me, both, for attacking us. That was okay with Vasco; he didn't care so long as his "sweet mamma" was loving. And I judge, from the way he went on about Miss Cooper, that Parker was getting his, too. I bet he didn't waste much time hunting for absent members.

So they had more drinks and the party was romping along, when there came a knock at the door. This was Jones. He had three men with him. Parker wouldn't tell me who they were—drunk as he was, you could see he was still scared—but I didn't need three guesses to identify their lodge buttons. When the Imperial Python of the Red Riders needed help, he hadn't gone out for Boy Scouts.

They told Vasco they wanted him outside. But Vasco was no fool. He refused to budge. So in they came.

"I want an apology and I want it quick," Parker said Jones said to Vasco. "This ain't New York and it ain't Italy and it ain't wherever you came from, dago. You heard what happened to Tucker's niggers. That ain't a patch alongside what's going to happen to you."

Either Vasco was just naturally dumb or he was honestly scared this time or he was too stubborn to speak.

"All right, grab him, boys!" said Jones and they grabbed him. Vasco didn't have a chance, Parker said. These guys were big guys and they were hard and they were going to take Vasco out then and there. Maybe to tar and feather him, maybe beat him up, maybe lynch him—I don't know. But I believe Parker when he said Vasco was whiter than he was blue.

Mrs. Boggs saved his skin. She got down on her knees and begged them, she said Vasco hadn't meant anything wrong and didn't know any better and was willing to apologize, she cried and blustered and carried on, and Jones just stood there—grinning, I bet—while the three men waited with ropes around Vasco. Finally, Jones took Mrs. Boggs in the bathroom and they had a big pow-wow. When they came out, Jones said, "All right, turn him loose," and Mrs. Boggs took Vasco in the bathroom. After a minute they came out and Vasco apologized to Jones and said he wanted to apologize to everybody. I guess by then he was willing to apologize to the Army and Navy. Jones said, "All right, boys, no party tonight," and the three men left and Jones with them.

I asked Parker if he knew Jones was a big gun in the Red Riders and he said he knew it now, all right. I asked him if he knew Mrs. Boggs was in the Red Riders, too, and he said he didn't care what she was in, Miss Rosy was his kinfolks, she was a fine woman and she would be a rich woman if she had her rights. He said his family was as good as any family in the county. He said they used to own all that land yon side of Chalk Creek where the Moodys lived now. He said the Moodys cheated them out of it and drove them and hounded them and brought them down to misery and starvation.

Miss Rosy, he said, never would have got into all that trouble when she was a girl if it hadn't been for the Moodys. He said she would never have had that baby and run away with that no 'count Boggs and been forced to sweat and slave for herself, but instead she would have had her rights and dressed in fine clothes and gone to boarding-school and kept company with rich men and married a rich man's son from Vesta like Leorah Moody. And he said he would have had his rights, too, and gone to the State University and owned a Packard car and had a pocketful of money and all the women he wanted, whether he married them or not.

As near as I could make out, all the trouble was over an old law-suit that was settled so long ago Parker wasn't even born and Miss Rosy was in pig-tails. On top of that, the fellow who went to law with the Moodys wasn't close kin to either Parker or Miss Rosy, he was a fourth cousin twice removed, but that didn't make any difference to Parker.

"No, sir, they stole our land," he said, "and don't you believe there ain't plenty of Parkers in this county that don't know it, and Cutshaws and Reynoldses and Wheelocks, too. If we all had our rights, those dang Moodys would be in the po' house."

He said Pendleton Moody was the uppitiest one of the lot and he was glad Miss Rosy called him out of his name this afternoon, but that Pendleton Moody was going to get his, all right, when he ran for superior court judge, and he would get it where the chicken got the ax. And there were plenty more, he said, who were going to get theirs, too, and he didn't mean only Moodys, but Todds and Mayfields and all that biggety crowd that called themselves society and snotted around insulting folks who were as good as they were and a heap better.

Then he went on with a lot more stuff about the people in this town and how the most righteous-acting were really the worst and the leading families were the lowest-down if you knew the truth. He could tell me things I wouldn't believe, he said, about immorality in this town, the gambling and love-making and hell-raising that went on among the rich folks, the husbands tom-catting off to Vesta and the wives riding out with other men as soon as their backs were turned, and their sons and daughters flaunting immorality at that country club where they swam buck naked, he'd heard.

But all that was going to be put a stop to, he said. A preacher had already preached a sermon about it and decent people were talking about doing something and he reckoned something was going to be done, too, because last Sunday, while that preacher was preaching, three masked, robed men came stomping down the aisle and handed the preacher five dollars and a note, "We are watching your good work and are behind you one hundred per cent." The note was signed "a thousand eyes," said Parker, but he bet he knew who wrote it.

I said I bet I did, too, and why wasn't he upstairs with the rest.

He hemmed and hawed and then he jerked out with it, half mad and half crying. It seems the party wasn't so cheerful after Jones and his boys left, so Miss Cooper suggested that he and she go to her room for a drink, where she had some in her bag. But just as they were weaving along the hall, who should bump into them but Jones?

"She said to excuse her a minute," said Parker, "and I reckoned she was going to ditch him soon as she could, so I decided to wait down here. You see, confidential between you and I, she's crazy about me."

I said it didn't pay to wait too long for any woman and maybe Miss Cooper had got sleepy and gone to bed.

"And there's where I'm going," I said, and I went.

We put out for Vesta next morning about eleven o'clock and we got there with less conversation than any five people ever dropped over a hundred and twenty miles before. The most of it was "Good-by!" and some of us didn't drop that much. The last I saw of Mirchison, the sun was shining bright on the trees and flowers and people in their go-to-meeting clothes ambling along the sidewalks and stopping to bow and chat in front of the old houses. And I thought, you're a nice little town, you're as pretty and sweet and friendly a little town as any of the thousands like you in this country, but there's ugliness in you, too, there's meanness and bitterness and strife, and God help you, Mirchison, when they pop!

CHAPTER FIVE

A T THE MOMENT I AM WRITING THIS STORY, THERE is big trouble in the world. There are persecutions and mass murders in Europe, war has come to end all hope of peace, and in this country the farms are barren, the cities hum with strikes, millions of people are jobless, business limps and groans, government tries to make the wheels go 'round and the only reason men do not damn government more is because they do not know where else to turn and they are afraid. They look at each other, shake their heads, talk of revolution here, wish for the old days and believe that never were days like this before.

Well, maybe there weren't, maybe human beings have changed, maybe their problems have, maybe we are headed for a new way of living and had better reach it soon or we die. Maybe this trouble is the biggest trouble the world has ever known. But I am not so sure. A man with influenza thinks he never felt worse in his life, certainly not that time he had the hives or the time he had the influenza before, when they called it grippe. Names change more than people or problems do, and we all forget yesterday so easily.

Do you remember 1919? We had plenty of trouble then. A million soldiers coming home from France and no place to put them. Labor facing a body-blow and Capital r'aring to sock it to them. Strikes in the East, the Wobblies raising hell in the West, the white-collar worker yelling over the High Cost of Living—"Why, a man's dollar ain't worth fifty cents!"—the stock market jiggling like a jumping-jack, mammas worried over the jazz-mad younger generation, the Republicans howling, "Back to normalcy!", the Democrats for Wilson's millennium, half the reformers claiming it was coming with prohibition, the rest with woman suffrage, while the die-hards predicted national ruin from both. The average man, reading the newspapers, believed the Bolsheviki were right around the corner and every beard hid a bomb.

If you don't believe things were that way, read Frederick Lewis Allen's "Only Yesterday." It's all there. He says, "It was an era of lawless and disorderly defense of law and order, of unconstitutional defense of the Constitution, of suspicion and civil conflict—in a very literal sense, a reign of terror."

In that day the Order of Red Riders was born—in thousands of Mirchisons all over the United States.

Down in our part of the world, the Negro took the place of the Bolsheviki. The Negro is a sizable bugabear at any time and right after the World War he was a grizzly. He was flocking north in hordes, leaving the southern employer shorthanded and sore. He was cocky on account of the war, the high wages it brought the Negro at home and the glory to the Negro that went. And this Negro soldier who had "seen the world," who had killed white men and fondled white women, was coming home a hero to his race and a menace to his white rulers. "If you don't watch out, the niggers are going to rise." And don't think this was just the talk of ignorant whites. In Atlanta, Birmingham, Vesta and every leading southern city, the first white citizens met with the first black citizens to organize safety committees against the wholesale race riots they surely expected.

"Look here," I said to Jones, "this story has dynamite in it and besides it isn't true."

We were in the crypt of propagation about a week after the fish fry and we were getting out the first number of Jones' weekly,

The Cyclops. He was the editor, but I did most of the work of copyreading and putting heads on stories written by the new men he'd hired.

"What's wrong with it?" he said, looking over my shoulder.

"It says that two million niggers have been demobilized 'after a year at the front and months of debauchery in the seraglios of Paris.' I don't know where this guy got his figures or his facts, but they're a lot of bull."

"I gave them to him," said Jones. "What's wrong with them?"

"Why, everybody knows there weren't but half a million niggers drafted and not more than two hundred thousand sent to France."

"There were two million registered for the draft, weren't they? It amounts to practically the same thing."

"Registering for the draft never got me to the seraglios of Paris. I wish it had. How many niggers do you suppose actually saw Paris?"

"Never mind—there were bawdy houses all over France and niggers went to them. Let the story ride."

"All right, but it looks to me like mighty dangerous stuff to be spreading around, inciting a lot of damn fools to violence."

"It won't," said Jones, grinning. "It'll just incite them to join the Red Riders. If they go out and scare a few niggers after that, it'll do the niggers good. We got a duty to the white people of this country to warn them."

"All right," I said, "it's your paper and you can run it like you want to. As far as I'm concerned, I'd just as leave write heads on these lies as the guff the *Courier* prints every time a banker has a birthday. But if you ask me, you're heading for grief."

"I didn't ask you," Jones said.

That's the way he was. He was getting more cocksure every day as the mails got bigger and bigger with the kick-ins from the King Cobras. He was getting bolder and bolder with the stories he printed and the propaganda he put out from the Supreme Palace.

He had four editions of *The Cyclops,* one for the South, one for the East, one for the Middle West and one for the Coast.

The southern edition carried yarns like this demobilization story, yarns about nigger agitators up North, the rape of some white girl, appointment of a colored postmaster, a speech by a northern politician, declaring the government ought to enfranchise the southern Negro by martial law. The speech was twenty years old, it was delivered when Cleveland ran for president, but you never could have told that from *The Cyclops.*

The eastern edition went heavy on the Jews, the middle-western bore down on the Catholics, the coast edition gave a good dose of the yellow peril and all of them played up the Bolsheviki.

If you believed what you read in *The Cyclops,* the Jews owned New York City, especially Wall Street and Broadway, they robbed the farmers downtown and ruined their daughters uptown, Jews were burrowing into every business in the country and grabbing off the dividends and the mortgages; if one hundred per cent Americans didn't watch out, they would be Jew-owned bank and boot; the Catholics, on the other hand, were in an ace of owning the Government, they already held most of the high offices, even the secretary to the President was a Catholic, Catholic chaplains had the run of the Army and Navy where Protestants were barred, the Knights of Columbus bossed our troops in Catholic France, they were trying to do the same thing over here, and, as everybody knew, if you were a K C, you took an oath of allegiance to the Pope and worked secretly to put him in the White House; as if all that wasn't bad enough, there were the Japs and Chinks, already taking the bread out of honest men's mouths by their cheap labor and planning to blow California to Kingdom

Come as soon as their spies, which were in every laundry and chop suey, gave the word. Should anything be left of the country after the Jews, the Catholics, the Japs, the Chinks and the niggers got through with it, the Reds were all set to take it over and enslave the surviving patriots.

Well, sir, that blooey may sound too ridiculous for anyone literate enough to read to swallow. But you can imagine what could happen when the rural free delivery left *The Cyclops* in a mail-box that got a Sears-Roebuck catalogue once a year and not much else, or when a King Cobra spread it on the molasses barrel before an audience that hadn't had anything to talk about since Bingham's barn burned.

You can imagine some pretty honest, hardworking fellow, who usually worries about nothing but laying by his crop and keeping his kids in shoes and his mortgage paid up and his stock fed, coming home to a wife who says, "John, did you know the Catholics are trying to get a law passed in Congress agin the farmer?" He tells her she's a fool woman and don't know what she's talking about and she says, "Oh, don't I? Well, here it is, right in the paper," and after he's made himself comfortable after supper, he reads where somebody with an Irish name has come out for a lower tariff on cottonseed oil, and though he never saw *The Cyclops* before, there's something awful convincing about the printed word wherever you find it. He still tells his wife she's a fool woman, but the next day at the store he hears somebody say the Catholics are trying to get control of politics and he speaks right up and says, "That's a fact, and they're aiming to lower the tariff on cotton and wheat and corn and hell knows what all—how come I know it?—I read it in the paper!" That leads to more argument and finally he, who wouldn't fear the devil if the devil came charging with a pitchfork across his own woodlot, goes home dreading a whole horde of distant devils who are plotting to take away his crop and his kids' shoes and his cattle and the house over his head. And if there's a King Cobra in the neighborhood—and there generally is if such talk's circulating around—that fellow is that King Cobra's meat.

There were plenty of fellows like that in America in the 1920's. Not all of them joined the Red Riders, but not all who did join were vicious men, either. They swore to defend the Flag, the Constitution and their Supreme Serpent—that great and good man, Simeon Sloat—and that's all they swore. And all it cost them to come into "blood brotherness" with one hundred per cent Americans like themselves, was ten dollars—just ten dollars. It was a cheap price to pay for salvation, to say nothing of the fun they were going to have, helling around nights instead of sitting at home hating their wives.

Maybe they wouldn't have jumped aboard so quick if they'd seen where their ten dollars were going, if they'd watched the King Cobras cutting four dollars to themselves, one dollar to the Terrible Tarantulas, and five dollars to the Supreme Treasury; or if they'd been in the Supreme Palace the day Mrs. Boggs slit a registered letter and out popped a check for $60,000, representing one Cobra's remittances for only three months' toiling in the vineyards of Indiana. Mrs. Boggs knocked the corks out of a case of liquor in the grand crypt that night and the Supreme Serpent couldn't crawl on his throne for a week.

The Cobras were go-getters, many of them salesmen for the war drives who'd lost their jobs after the Armistice. They knew how to get money, big money, and if they weren't honest, they learned that honesty paid, for Jones organized a spy system inside the Red Riders as feared by the Tarantulas and Cobras as outsiders feared them. If a Cobra got drunk with a dame once too often, and bragged too loud, he was liable to lose more than his job. But that was later on, when Jones had some of the toughest muggs in the United States on his payroll.

Usually, he handled the boys like any executive handles his sales staff. He had the Tarantulas and the star Cobras come in regularly to headquarters. He gave them "pep talks" and outlined arguments to use on prospects. Mostly this was stuff too hot for *The Cyclops* to print: Jones was taking no chances on sending obscene matter through the mails.

He instructed them to go after the "big men" in a community first. "Go after the preachers. Go after the police. If you get the law and the church lined up, you've got the town." Nobody knows how many cops became Red Riders, how many chiefs of police, sheriffs, deputies, bailiffs, public prosecutors and even judges. Nobody knows how many a little preacher, thanking the Lord for that unexpected contribution to his church from the "invisible eye," threw in his lot with the "veiled legion" who were watching his "good work" and "approved" it. Jones hired half a dozen preachers—rip-roaring evangelists who knew how to scare congregations, whether with Hell or the Pope—to tour the Dens and Lairs and lecture on "blood brotherness," one hundred per cent Americanism and the various dangers menacing white civilization.

But the best shot in his bag was Simeon Sloat himself. He built up Doc Sloat in *The Cyclops* as a second Messiah, a sort of amalgam of Socrates, Moses, Robert E. Lee, Andrew Carnegie and the Holy Ghost. The Supreme Serpent's life-long dream, said *The Cyclops*, had been to found an order that would guide mankind out of chaos into universal brotherhood. The vision had come to him as a little boy walking across the battlefield of Gettysburg. It had haunted him through the classic halls of the world's greatest institutions of learning, it had been his sword in war, his scepter in the strategies of finance, his mission in private audiences with the crowned heads of Europe. Returning to America disappointed but undaunted, Dr. Sloat had decided to pin his hope on the rugged Anglo-Saxon and to devote his vast fortune to the promulgation of Anglo-Saxon ideals. The entire Sloat millions were behind the Red Riders, (membership fees scarcely paid the cost of enrollment), and this kindly, noble, beneficent, yet fiery, gallant and astute old gentleman sat godlike in the grand crypt of the Supreme Palace, immersed in his plans for scientific and eleemosynary endowments (which shortly would be announced), while he directed with all-seeing wisdom the progress and fulfillment of his staggering conception. Some of the best fun I ever had was writing those Sloat stories, which were always illustrated with specially posed photos of the Doc in full regalia. He was a good model, for more often than not when he faced the camera he was so boiled he couldn't blink.

The only drawback to building up the Doc was that occasionally Jones had to put him on parade. Whenever a new Cobra or Tarantula came to town, he always wanted to see Dr. Sloat. He'd heard about him and he'd read about him and so had all the boys back home. He wasn't going to return to the sticks without a look at Dr. Sloat and, if possible, the old gentleman's blessing. Privately, I dare say, a lot of them doubted Dr. Sloat's existence and wanted assurance as well as their cut of the take.

If Sloat was particularly drunk that day or the visiting King Cobra wasn't awfully insistent, Jones tried to duck the business. Dr. Sloat was closeted with the Supreme Reptilate (Red Rider for directorate), or Dr. Sloat was in Washington conferring with a Very Important Person. But if there was no way out of it, Jones trusted to his props and the Doc's famed ability to orate from a coma. His props included heavy draperies, trick lights, a fall-proof throne, costumes and incense-pots. Usually, too, he gave the Cobra a couple of drinks before the audience, a swallow of corn liquor being the perfect foil to the smell of corn liquor.

I never had the luck to witness one of those séances—after all, I was an outlaw and a lot I learned during those days was office talk—but I can see it in my mind's eye. I can see your King Cobra, a little flustered from his drinks and the ballyhoo Jones had fed him and all those dizzy dames he has to pass enroute to the grand crypt, barging in there not knowing what to expect. The stage is set for him. The room is dark as Egypt except for the flicker of red and green lights. Incense half blinds him and half dopes him. He's announced—"King Cobra of the Jungle of the Southeast, Den of Alabama, Lair of Tuscaloosa!"—and right there he's put in character and has to play their way. Up rises the Supreme Serpent, if he's sober enough, from a pitch-black perch you'd never suspect was an over-stuffed chair covered with cheese-cloth and fitted with a safety-belt. Sloat—I believe I told you—was six feet two and all bone and gristle. In a crimson robe with black hood, the special vestment of his office, he was nobody's clown. If your Cobra is expecting Santa Claus, he isn't disappointed, he's astonished and thrilled. You can't blame him if he bends the knee. And after Sloat waves the silver caduceus and uncorks the bull-bass, your Cobra goes away from there considerably hypnotized. Chances are he won't remember a word of what he heard, but while he was hearing it, it sounded swell. I know it did, for once I had to copy out part of it for the Doc. It went like this:

"My brother, we welcome you into a fellowship whose watchword is 'God give us men!' The Order of Red Riders demands strong minds, great hearts, true faith and ready hands. Men whom the lust of office does not kill. Men whom the spoils of office cannot buy. Men who possess opinions and a will. Men who love honor, men who will not lie. Men who can stand before

a demagogue and damn his treacherous flatteries without winking. Tall men, sun-crowned, who live above the fog in public duty
and in private thinking. For while the rabble with their thumb-
worn creeds mingle in selfish strife, freedom weeps, wrong rules
the land and waiting justice sleeps. Such is the code of our noble
Order. Brother, I greet you in blood brotherness, by the unfailing
sacred bond of Boa!"

The day Doc Sloat reeled that off to me, I said, "Doctor,
haven't I read something like that before somewhere?"

"Impossible, son—it came to me in a vision in my sleep. I
dreamed I stood on Crag Mountain, alone, and those words
appeared in the heavens in letters of fire. They were burned
indelibly on my brain. Nevertheless, you might write 'em out for
me so Brother Jones can read 'em. Have you got a chaw of tobacco
on you, son? That admirable woman, Mrs. Boggs, confiscated my
last plug."

I wrote them out, willing to bet he was the world's champion
liar, and sure enough, next day at the office when I got down
Bartlett, there it was on Page 730, "God give us men," by Josiah
Gilbert Holland, 1819-1881, verbatim except where the Doc had
stuck in the Red Riders stuff. He had swiped that whole piece as
coolly as Mrs. Boggs hooked his plug.

If he hadn't been such a bleary old buck, I would have liked
him, for there's charm in a man who lies to your face and knows
you know he's lying. I've had the Doc tell me five versions of the
renascence of the Red Riders, all different, all picturesque and all
lies. The one I liked best was about the death of Eli P. Manton.
He was shot, according to the Doc, in a duel with a renegade
Confederate cavalry officer, when the Doc was Manton's second.
When they took him home, bleeding from a gaping hole in his
chest, he excluded his weeping family from the room, summoned
Sloat and, with the death-rattle in his throat, revealed to him the

secrets of the Red Riders, charged him to carry on the Order and knighted him with the silver caduceus. "And there, my boy, it is!" the Doc would declaim, "General Manton's own!" though every schoolboy knew Eli P. Manton died of apoplexy at the Cotton States Exposition in 1895 and everybody in the Palace knew that Doc Sloat was always losing his caduceus and the one on his desk at the moment was at least his fifth.

At that, I never believed Sloat was the same stripe of crook as Jones, for example. The worst you could say of him was that he started something. His intentions were no blacker than any wildcat stock promoter's and they may have been a whole lot better. When Jones flattered and bullied and scared him along, Sloat didn't know what it was all about and I don't doubt he sincerely thought he was saving the country, and got to believing half the hokum in his boozy head, including his own stories, and enjoyed being Supreme Serpent, and worked at the job, and accepted his share of the gravy as his just and honest due.

You take that business of the caduceus. It wasn't really silver, it was lead, and I suppose you could have bought them a dime a dozen. But the Doc loved his caduceus, he wanted to carry it wherever he went and he figured out a way to do it, too, by slipping the caduceus into an umbrella case. A man can't very well flourish an umbrella and a cane at the same time, so the Doc had to give up his "sword cane," which shows you how proud he was of being head man of the Red Riders, for the "sword cane," though it actually was hollow, didn't hide steel at all but a glass tube grooved to contain one jigger of whiskey.

The trouble was that the Doc would get paralyzed drunk and leave his caduceus around. He would leave it in saloons and other public places, and if the finder didn't hold it up and holler, "Whose is this fairy's wand?" he was so disgusted because it wasn't an umbrella that he chucked it out with the garbage.

The Doc always swore that somebody stole the caduceus. But that didn't go down with Jones. He got madder every time a new caduceus was lost; he said Sloat was ruining the dignity of the Order and costing it a mint of money.

He began to get sore at the Doc, too, about his singing. Before the Supreme Palace was moved to the Commerce Building, the Doc had confined his bass to oratory when he was stewed, but after Jones started his expansion program and brought in a lot of new talent, the Doc met Gabe Trippy and oratory took a back seat. Reverend Gabriel Trippy was one of the preachers Jones hired. He had been a singing evangelist— "Golden Gabe," they called him—and before that a circuit rider in the Blue Ridge Mountains, where the Sacred Harpers and the Christian Harmonists travel miles to all-day singings. I guess Golden Gabe knew more hymn tunes than any man alive. Whenever he was in town, the Doc would invite him into the grand crypt and they would hist a few and then they would start on the hymns.

Gabe would line them out, the Doc would take it up, pretty soon they would both hit together and when they were well lathered up on something like "The Sweet By and By" or "Rescue the Perishing," you could hear them for blocks. They had one hymn that was their favorite. It went, "There is power, power, wonder-working power, in the blood of the Lamb," and it was a swinging tune with the accent strong on the "powers." But the Doc sang it wrong one time—"There is blood, blood, precious, precious blood, in the power of the Lamb!" he sang it—and they agreed the hymn sounded better that way and from then on they always sang it wrong, with the accent on the "bloods."

Jones finally raised hell about the hymn-singing. He said it was irreligious and blasphemous, as well as undignified and bad for office discipline, and he said he was going to fire Trippy. For once, the Doc stood up to him and there was a row the whole Palace heard. Jones went to Mrs. Boggs.

"Look here," he said, "we've got to do something. We can't have that pair of old bums caterwauling day and night in the grand crypt. The first thing you know the cops'll be on our neck. I thought you promised to make him cut down on the booze."

Mrs. Boggs hadn't been so cordial to Jones since the fish fry; she was showing up red-eyed in the mornings and the story in the office was that she was out every night with Vasco.

"Who gives him booze when you want something out of him?" she said. "The old gentleman gets lonely back there with nothing to do. What harm is it if he and Reverend Trippy hum a little?"

Jones blew up.

"For the love of God," he yelled, "what is this, the Salvation Army? I've a good mind to throw the whole lot of you out on your necks!"

Mrs. Boggs just looked at him and for a fat woman she could look thinner and colder and flintier than a skull.

"You'll do what?" she said.

"You heard me!" blustered Jones.

Mrs. Boggs turned to her secretary—"Miss Dibble, fetch me that steel box in the safe and call up Mr. Bellis"—and Jones went a kind of a dirty green and got up and gave a groan and walked out.

Mr. Bellis was Mrs. Boggs' lawyer and I suppose the steel box contained something on Jones. Maybe the charter. Maybe a signed agreement. Maybe his note for money she'd loaned him. Maybe worse. Miss Dibble wouldn't tell me. As long as I worked for the Red Riders, I never found out what the arrangement was among those three, Sloat, Jones and Boggs, how much they got and which way they split. I tried to pump Miss Dibble, but I don't believe she knew. I doubt if anybody knew.

The feud over the singing didn't stop there, though. They could out-bluff Jones and out-yell him, but they couldn't out-smart him. One day he called me into his office and handed me a story for *The Cyclops*.

"I want you to rewrite this, Dudley. All the facts are there, but it lacks sympathy, it lacks appeal. Give it the old Dudley touch. You know-hearts and flowers."

I read the story and it said the Order of Red Riders, in admiration and gratitude to their Supreme Serpent for his years of unrewarded toil, had decided to present him with a home. The home was to be a white marble mansion on the outskirts of Vesta, it would cost $75,000, it would be a haven for Dr. Sloat and a monument and a mecca for Red Riders all over the world, and the money to build it would come from public donations.

"Who's going to feel grateful enough to donate a dime to the Doc?" I wanted to know.

"The Red Riders, of course. You didn't think we'd get it from the B'nai B'rith, did you? Why, there ain't a Lair in the country won't go over the top for Dr. Sloat. The people of the United States got the giving habit in the war and they're not broke of it yet. If all these colleges can raise endowments, I reckon the Red Riders can give enough to house their Supreme Serpent properly."

It was a fact that even little jerkwater colleges were hiring "experts" to put over drives like the war drives, and they were getting the money, too. It sounds crazy, after all the bleeding and bulldozing people had gone through during the war, but that's the crazy way things were then.

"But why a mansion?" I said. "A good 'still would do. Aren't you getting mighty generous to Dr. Sloat all of a sudden?"

Jones winked. "He won't need but one room and that'll be down in the cellar where he can sing his fool head off. The rest will be for other officers and—lodge work."

"Where you going to build this mansion?"

"It's already built—'Smith's Folly'!"

Everybody in Vesta knew "Smith's Folly." Jasper Smith was one of our rich crackpots, of which every city has a few. His particular mania was his name. He was prouder to be a Smith than Cabots are to be Cabots, he organized societies and reunions of Smiths, he traced the Smith tree back to Alfred the Great, he loved all Smiths and hated anybody who poked fun at a Smith. Once, when the papers said a woman in Chicago had petitioned the courts to change her name from Smith to Smythe, Jasper hopped the next train north and sued for an injunction to stop her. His big inspiration was to build a sixty-story skyscraper as a sort of international Smithery, with club rooms on every floor for the Smiths of every state and every country. But he died intestate before the job was well started and his next of kin, whose name was Williams, had been trying to sell "Smith's Folly" ever since. Two stories and a lot of scaffolding, it loomed up on a hill ten miles out of town like a white hippopotamus under the skeleton of a tent.

Here was a sure-enough ready-made Palace for the Supreme Serpent. I could see where Jones not only was fixing to sell the Doc down the river where he couldn't bother anybody, but that probably he already had an option on "Smith's Folly" and was all set to unload it on the Red Riders for three times what he paid for it. But you couldn't have told the Doc that if you'd had the heart.

He was as proud and pleased with the prospect as a kid on Christmas Eve. "And do you know what they're going to install, son?" he said to me. "An organ!—yes, sir, none of your new-fangled pianos or phonographs, but a regular, old-fashioned organ.

You'll have to come out sometime and hear her when she gets going." I could tell by the look in his eye that, whatever magnificence Jones had in mind, the Doc was seeing one of those parlor melodeons you still run across away out in the country. "Why, son," he said, "I haven't heard an organ like that in fifty years. My poor old sainted mother used to play one. Her favorite hymn was 'Amazing grace! how sweet the sound, that saved a wretch like me!' "

I believe he was telling the truth for the first time I ever heard him.

"I'll be there," I said, and I meant it. But before the workmen started on "Smith's Folly" something happened that left me very much on its outside looking in.

CHAPTER SIX

T HE CITY DESK TELEPHONE RANG AT SEVEN o'clock, which was an early hour for anyone to call, when the staff was just straggling in to work. Deadwyler answered and it was police—a murder. "Take it," he said to me. "If it's any good, we'll hurry up the first edition."

It wasn't any good. A motorcycle cop, riding the Lakeside Road at dawn, found a man's body in the bushes. Apparently he'd bled to death from stab wounds after a struggle, for the ground was trampled and a hundred yards down the road was a bloody clasp-knife. Near the body were bloody strips of sacking and a piece of cloth cut like a mask. A union card in his pocket identified the dead man as Frank Turk, machinist's helper, 432 Pickett Street.

This was mysterious enough—there were few gangsters and no "rides" in our city—but you can't make big mysteries out of machinists' helpers with addresses in the mill district. I wrote three paragraphs and went down to the soda fount for breakfast.

When I got back, the story was a little hotter. The cops had picked up a suspect five miles from the scene of the crime, walking towards the city, his clothes and hands bloody and his talk wild. They were grilling him and we were to stand by for a confession.

The confession came in time for the first edition.

Nathan Plotz, 42, proprietor of a soft-drink stand at 1091 Carmine Street, said he was closing his place at midnight when an automobile drove up and someone called his name. When he walked over to the car, four men, who had gotten out on the far side, jumped him. He did not recognize them because they were masked. They overpowered him, gagged and blindfolded him and forced him into the car. He did not know how long they rode, he was too frightened to guess. When the car finally stopped, his fear was so great that, as they dragged him from the car, he shook himself free, managed to open his knife and struck blindly in the dark. One man, at least, fought him, but when this one fell, he ran. He did not know where the other men went or, for hours of wandering, where he himself was. That was all, so help him God—he never knew a Frank Turk and he had never seen the dead man before, he was poor, he had no enemies and he was at as much of a loss to account for the kidnaping as the police were.

"It sounds screwy to me," said Deadwyler. "Tell Rosser to talk to that guy himself."

I 'phoned Rosser, our police reporter, and in half an hour he 'phoned back. "I didn't get much out of him, he's a thick-headed German, but I believe he's telling the truth. He did let go one thing. He said about a week ago he got an anonymous letter, threatening him. He didn't pay much attention to it because it didn't make sense and he thought somebody was kidding him. He tore it up. But he does remember it was signed 'One Thousand Eyes.' And oh, yes, here's something else—the police say those bloody rags they thought were a sack had armholes like for a shirt or a sweater. A long red sweater."

I hung up and I sat staring at my notes and then I went over to Deadwyler.

"Look here," I said, "I want to go out and work this story. I think there's more to it and I've got a hunch where to look."

"Okay—but it's a heluva time of day for it—give her my love," he said.

"You're just jealous," I said, and I went out.

It wasn't ten o'clock, but Jones was already in his office and I thought he looked flustered. I decided to play the hunch as a sure thing.

"Well, well, the Red Riders of Vesta Lair, Jungle of the Southeast, didn't do so well on their first crusade, did they?"

"What do you mean?"

"I mean one fat Heinie can lick the whole bunch. Too bad Mr. Turk resisted. He ought've had his horse."

"I don't know what you're talking about," Jones said.

"What!" I said. "You didn't hear? I would've thought the cops had been around before now. I'm talking about the business out on Lakeside Road last night. Somebody decided to get tough with a sixty per cent American named Plotz—runs a joint on Carmine Street—and they took him out in a car to beat him up. Plotz was like the Chinaman in the story—he didn't like it. So he cut one of 'em to death."

"What's that got to do with the Red Riders?"

"Oh, not a thing—only the guy that got killed wore a red robe and I shouldn't wonder, when they come to piece it together, if it didn't have cobra specs on it. Furthermore, Plotz got a threatening letter. It was signed 'One Thousand Eyes.' "

Jones looked sick; he shook his head, trying to grin.

"Come off it," I said. "I'm not telling you anything you don't know. The boys must have called you hours ago to break the sad news."

"I give you my word, Dudley," he declared, "I never heard of this until you mentioned it. And I still don't see why the Red Riders should be dragged into it. You know we don't stand for any violence. Of course, if somebody takes advantage of the Order and masquerades in our regalia, we can't help it, can we?"

"So that's the alibi," I said. "Well, if you're so innocent, what was Steve Timberlake doing around here this morning? I passed him coming out and he looked worried. He's Cobra or something of Vesta Lair, isn't he?"

"You'll have to ask Mr. Timberlake that."

"I will—but meantime I'm asking you."

"Asking me what? I told you I don't know anything."

"I'm a reporter. I want a statement from the Red Riders."

He sat back and laughed till his tongue almost hung out.

"No, you don't! We have no statement to make. The matter simply doesn't concern us."

I got up.

"Well," I said, "I guess I'll have to get my own story and write it my own way."

"What do you mean by that?"

"I mean, from what I know, it looks to me like the Red Riders flung a boomerang. It's a good story when a man bites a snake."

"You can't write that story; it's libelous."

"It won't be the way I'll write it—the old Dudley touch, you know."

He looked at me with all his red fox in his eyes.

"I said you can't write it. Aren't you forgetting you're a salaried employee here?"

"You mean I was a salaried employee here—I quit ten seconds ago," I said and I walked out. I wasn't being noble; you're a newspaper man first if you're any kind of a newspaper man at all, and besides, I never did like that bastard Jones.

I got back to the office about noon and I told Joe Deadwyler all I knew and all I suspected.

"You think they went after him because he's a German, then?" he said.

"No, I don't. After I left Jones, I went to 1091 Carmine Street and took a look at Mrs. Plotz. Their stand is away out, almost to the city limits. It's just this side of the Bennett Bag and Spinning Mills. Pickett Street, where Turk lived, is out that way, too. The cops had been there ahead of me and Mrs. Plotz wouldn't talk, but she looked plenty and, Joe, she didn't look like any German hausfrau. She looked fly. You know—one of those hard-cheeked, restless dames who paint everything but their ears. From what I could gather, she tends store for Plotz half the day and the other half she's home. I don't know which door he came in, but I'll lay a bet she had a sweetie, and if his name wasn't Turk, he was one of Turk's pals. It's as simple for a Red Rider to call out his gang to save his coozie as his country."

Deadwyler thought, always a tough job for a city editor.

"Will she stand for a picture?"

"Why not?—she's a dame."

"Wait a minute, I'll have to take this up with Mr. Roberts."

I waited while he talked to Roberts, the managing editor, and I waited while they both went downstairs and talked to old Colonel Cronkhite. When Deadwyler came back, he looked sour.

"We can't print it."

"Why not?"

"Well, to begin with, you can't prove anything. You just think this letter signed 'One Thousand Eyes' came from the Red Riders. You just think that bloody shirt may have an insignia on it and, if it has, that it belonged to a Red Rider. You just think Turk or one of the others wore it and, if they did, that makes them Red Riders. And you just think they were working off a private grudge, which, if they were, sort of relieves the Red Riders of responsibility."

"All right—I just think. But turn me loose on this story and I'll guarantee to bring you proof."

Deadwyler shook his head. "Nothing doing. Colonel Cronkhite says that's the business of the police. If the police make charges involving the Red Riders, we'll publish them."

"Hell! Half the police *are* Red Riders! They won't make charges. Hell," I said, "I've known Colonel Cronkhite not to be so pussy-footing. Why, on the Sorsby murder case he had us chasing our pants off trying to scoop the police!"

"That was different. That was a big murder. They don't regard this as a big murder. You can't get the town excited over a delicatessen dealer bushwhacking a mechanic."

I didn't have much left to say.

"Look here, don't be an ass," Deadwyler said. "Can't you see? The story's unimportant and you're stirring up more trouble than it's worth. If somebody killed a Shriner, the paper wouldn't go after the Masons. We don't know anything against these Red Riders. They seem to be a second-rate lodge, but the members may be perfectly decent and respectable and they may be subscribers to the *Courier,* too. Roberts called up Joe Briggs at the City Hall and Joe said they were all right. He said that old jaybird, Doc Sloat, was behind the thing, but he said the Red Riders had gotten pretty strong and a lot of politicians and influential men were in it."

"You're not telling me anything," I said, thinking of Steve Timberlake, who was an alderman.

"All right—that's the way it is. You can't expect the *Courier* to attack a lot of prominent citizens and maybe get in a libel suit because Joe Doakes laid Jim Brown's wife."

I went back to my desk and I felt pretty blue. To be honest about it, I didn't grieve so much over missing the chance to take a poke at the old O-R-R. The O-R-R had been pretty good to me in dollars and cents and a man's considered a rat who turns on the hand that fed him. Besides, I didn't feel any moral or social obligations, then, to fight the O-R-R. I knew they were a bunch of phonies, but as I've said before, what they were doing, even the racial and religious propaganda, seemed no worse than what half the secret societies and churches themselves were doing—protecting their own. But it was a good story—that's what griped me—a story to go out and get and print no matter who it hit or hurt—and I wanted my paper to have it. Hell, I'd gone after it for no other reason but that it was a good story—and what was my reward? Thirty dollars a week shot to hell.

Well, I got over being sore—a kid at Magnolia brained his whole family with an ax that afternoon and they gave me the assignment—and I got over regretting the thirty dollars. Considering the nature of the job and the objections to Jones as a boss, I was glad to be shut of it. And things began to happen soon afterward that would have made it impossible to hold the job and be a good newspaper man, too.

They didn't happen in Vesta—apparently one dead Red Rider had put the fear of God into the living, or else the Supreme Palace talked turkey to the local boys. Plotz went free on a plea of self-defense, nobody appeared to testify against him and the Red Riders weren't mentioned at the coroner's inquest. If they paid Turk's funeral expenses—which I heard they did—the record didn't show it, and if members of Vesta Lair rode by night any more, they must have confined their shindigs to niggers or folks that didn't carry clasp-knives, for the capital of "blood brotherness" was singularly innocent of violence for many, many months.

You couldn't say the same for the rest of the country. Gradually, and then so suddenly it was like the explosion of an epidemic, masked mayhem became common the length and breadth of the United States. A white man was tarred and feathered in Texas, two white women were flogged in Arkansas, the states of Florida, Delaware, Ohio and Nevada reported whippings and in California "a mob of armed and masked vigilantes" almost beat to death a fellow who appeared to have been guilty of nothing but shiftlessness.

I say the thing was "gradual," and it was, and I say it was "sudden," and it was. It was gradual because, since the victims of these outrages were mostly obscure and their assailants stopped short of murder, the incidents were frequently glossed over or suppressed by the local papers and for a long time the big press associations didn't consider them important enough to carry on their wires. It was sudden because suddenly the press of the United States woke up to the significance of the outrages.

You've seen a thing like that happen often. A "test-tube baby" is headlined in New York and at once "test-tube babies" are news everywhere. A boy climbs a tree in Kansas and immediately treesitters fill the front pages of the nation. Or a Senator "dunks" his food and not a paper in the land but doesn't trot out its dunkers and non-dunkers.

In the case of the "masked menace," as the newspapers came to call it, the whippings had been going on here and there for months with no more national to-do over them than if they'd been so many fist fights on Main Street. Then, in Oklahoma, a whipping was definitely linked to the Red Riders and the same week, in a town in Pennsylvania, a parade of Red Riders ended in a small riot. The metropolitan dailies began to play up these stories and, before long, he was a poor correspondent, no matter how small his town, who couldn't discover a whipping or at least the burning of a fiery serpent to sell to *The New York Times*. The correspondents weren't above laying any crime of violence and mystery to the Red Riders if there was nobody else to lay it to. Probably the Red Riders got the blame for much they didn't do, but certainly they did plenty.

If you read the newspapers widely in those days, you noticed a peculiar thing about those outrages—the victims seldom were Negroes despite the anti-Negro creed of the O-R-R. They were seldom Jews or Catholics. They were white, they were Protestant, they were native-born. Sometimes the victim was the town bootlegger or the town drunkard, or, in the case of the women, the town trollop, for the O-R-R was outwardly as moral as Anthony Comstock. But usually the victim was some poor nonentity like Plotz and the motive for the outrage was a mystery. I don't doubt, could you have fathomed it, you would have found a private grudge at the bottom of most of them. The rancors and meannesses in the Mirchisons of America were having their innings under the red hood.

You would have noticed another peculiar thing—many of the newspapers played down the outrages instead of playing them up and some did not publish them at all. Those were the communities where the O-R-R was strong. The editors were afraid to antagonize a large and powerful group. Most editors are just as fearful of antagonizing the Jews and Catholics. In communities where the O-R-R was strong and the Jews and Catholics, too, I imagine the editors did some painful squirming.

The O-R-R was not strong in Vesta. Nor did the Vesta papers, which are as brave and intelligent and enterprising as the average paper anywhere, suppress the stories as they began to trickle in over the wire. They printed them, even when they mentioned the O-R-R, and usually they sent a reporter to the Palace and got a statement from Jones and printed that, too. The statement always deplored the outrage and disclaimed responsibility for it and suggested that "unscrupulous parties masquerading as Red Riders" did the deed.

"You'll print that slop when you wouldn't print a real story when you had it," I said to Deadwyler.

He just laughed.

The fact was that the O-R-R was a laughing matter in Vesta. In a city where Sloat and Jones were known as frauds to hundreds of people and where roughnecks only belonged to their order, no one above the grade of roughneck took the order seriously. Vestians had smiled when they first saw those pictures of the "sons of the New South" in hoods and robes, and now they laughed at the notion of old Doc Sloat as a "masked menace." When they read the stories, they just couldn't connect a beating in Illinois with the construction going on at that freak Smith place out the River Road. A man in Georgia or Alabama, I've noticed, is mighty indifferent to quivering, bloody flesh in Chicago. We'll take care of our own crimes; you take care of yours—that's the South's attitude.

But pretty soon, if you went to New York, for example, and you met somebody and he heard you were from Vesta, he immediately asked you about the Red Riders. That's all the name of Vesta meant to those Northerners, you discovered, and the discovery made you a little sore. Oh, sure, you told him, you belonged to the Red Riders and went nigger-hunting every night and usually ate a black baby for breakfast. But if he insisted on being serious and you told him the Red Riders didn't amount to a hill of beans in Vesta and were considered a big joke there, he looked at you as though to say, "Ah, the secret stuff, eh? So you're one of them—and probably a King Cobra."

Mac Kelly came back from a vacation in New York and said he felt like a combination of Monte Cristo and Gyp the Blood all the time he was there. A dame in a night club called him her Terrible Tarantula and he got in three fights with Jews and he said he was about ready to join the Red Riders now if he hadn't been before. People denounced the Red Riders and said how low and contemptible they were, but they were awed and fascinated by the Red Riders, too—even sensible people. And people in Vesta, though they laughed, began to get on the defensive and to excuse and uphold the Red Riders just because the North was so down on them.

Then, just as all the hullabaloo began to die out and it seemed as if the "masked menace" might go the way of the tree-climbers and the flagpole-sitters and the other sensations Americans get excited about for nine days, the Red Riders were no longer a joke to Vesta. They became a big problem.

A small thing set off the powder train. In Pineyville, a little town near the center of the state, a Negro preacher preached a Christmas sermon. He preached about a new Star in the East and three Wise Men following it and a Babe in a manger. Only the Babe in his sermon was not white, it was black; the Black Messiah that was to save the black race and rule the world.

Well, you might think the colored congregation of a little cross-roads church in deep Dixie could have their dream of a black Jesus without endangering white civilization, but that evidently wasn't the way the whites of Pineyville felt, for the next Sunday night, while the preacher and his flock were shouting their hallelujahs, fire broke out all around them and as they tore running and screaming into the open, a fusillade of bullets met them and three were killed and several wounded and a woman and her child were burned to death. And there wasn't much doubt as to who did the deed this time; witnesses saw them driving away in their red robes and on the door of Pineyville courthouse next morning was nailed a proclamation, boasting that worse would happen to black blasphemers from now on, and the proclamation was signed O-R-R.

Stories like that can't be soft-pedaled. Vesta and Margana and cities as far away as Atlanta and Birmingham sent reporters and photographers to Pineyville, and I was one of them and I saw

the charred and riddled bodies and talked to the county prosecutor, who said no stone would be left unturned to apprehend
the guilty parties, and I watched the usual course of justice as it
unfolds after the mob has acted in the Pineyvilles of the world—
the coroner's inquest and the verdict of "first degree murder at
the hands of parties unknown," the prosecutor and the sheriff
disappearing half the day and getting gruffer and more mysterious as the "arrests at any moment" don't develop, the meeting of
the grand jury, the failure to return indictments, and finally—
nothing, but the hard eyes of silent, red-necked men who needn't
speak for strangers to realize it will be healthier to go back where
they came from.

The Southern papers ran the Pineyville story for a week,
including the usual disclaimer from the Supreme Palace in
Vesta, and a number of the better ones published editorials
denouncing lawlessness. Then they would have let a bad business drop if the Northern press had allowed them to. But the
Northern press, which is never so happy as when one convict
escapes from a Georgia chain-gang while fifteen gangsters are
being paroled from Sing Sing, was baying after the "barbarous
South" like the hounds after Little Eva. The Negro preacher
had fled north from Pineyville, his picture and interviews filled
the New York papers, the New York radicals held indignation
meetings and the New York columnists marched John Brown's
body from the grave. Sacco and Vanzetti were in jail in Boston,
but not for five years would their sympathizers harry the state
of Massachusetts into killing them. The South was the patsy of
the moment.

Still, there wasn't much for the North to do about it. There
were no Scottsboro boys to be boosted toward the chair by their
Northern friends, and all their fury couldn't raise those poor
Pineyville darkies from the dead. There was but one shining

mark left to shoot at in the Pineyville tragedy and one New York paper, the *Sphere,* determined to hit it hard.

Some people will tell you that the *Sphere's* exposé of the Red Riders was a mere circulation stunt and some will say it was the fearless and public-spirited act of a great crusading newspaper. I'm not going to argue the point. My guess is both; I've noticed that the circulation departments of newspapers are never exactly reticent when the editorial departments go high-minded, but newspapers are not gentlemen and nobody expects them not to capitalize their own righteousness and courage.

We in Vesta—that is to say, the newspaper crowd—knew what the *Sphere* was plotting months before the first gun was fired. I hadn't been back from Pineyville a week when I was called down to Colonel Cronkhite's office. Chester Steward, the editor of the *Morning Star,* was there, and George Upton, who runs the *Blade* for A. B. Gerard, the millionaire who owns papers all over the United States. In a newspaper town as highly competitive as Vesta you don't get the big shots of the three dailies together for anything less important than a printers' strike, but it soon developed that the subject of this powwow wasn't labor troubles, it was the Red Riders. Colonel Cronkhite wanted to know what I knew about the Red Riders and I told them and I didn't dress it up or play it down.

Well, before I was good and through, the door opened and Mr. Roberts ushered in Harvey P. Douglas, the president of the Vesta board of trade.

I don't like Harvey P. Douglas and none of the newspaper boys do. He's a mean little man who thinks his speeches come down from Sinai and rate as much attention as God's, but he controls the biggest advertising account in Vesta and whenever he belches we open up the front page.

He bustled in, shaking hands with Colonel Cronkhite and the others and giving me his always-glad-to-see-the-boys smile. He said, "Well, well, Colonel, what's this, what's this? I had a very important engagement, but I broke it when Roberts 'phoned. What's the bad news?—let's have it."

Colonel Cronkhite is the keenest old gentleman alive, but he doesn't like to be rushed, by Harvey P. Douglas or anyone else.

"Sit down, Harvey," he said. "Sit down and have a cigar. We're here on pretty serious business, I'm afraid. Looks like the Pineyville mess all over again."

Douglas bit his cigar and spat the bit-off end on the rug.

"Impossible! It can't be, it mustn't be. We've had enough publicity of that sort and I certainly trust you gentlemen aren't thinking of printing any more. In my opinion, you went too far as 'twas."

Colonel Cronkhite didn't say anything, and George Upton, who takes his orders from A. B. Gerard and nobody else, blew smoke. Chester Steward is the greatest pacificator—and so is his paper—that ever found the middle of the road in a storm. He said, "Unfortunately, Harvey, it isn't we who are thinking of publishing anything more; it's the *New York Sphere*. The *Sphere* is planning an exposé of the Red Riders."

Harvey P. Douglas turned pinker than pork.

"Damn those fellows!" he exploded. "I wish I'd never heard of them—they're hurting the town!"

He meant the Red Riders, for he went on to cuss them for a pack of thugs and thieves that weren't worth the gunpowder to blow them up. If he had his way, he said, he would run them out of Vesta exactly as they ran the niggers out of Pineyville.

"Oh, I don't know, Harvey," put in Colonel Cronkhite in that dry way of his. "They're getting Vesta more national advertising than your 'Come to Vesta' campaign did."

"Damn bad advertising, too!"

"Our friend, Reeves, at the bank, tells me they're his third biggest depositor," remarked George Upton.

Douglas snorted, but he looked surprised. I don't suppose he considered the First National Bank ever had any depositor except the H. P. Douglas Company.

"They ought to be exposed just the same," he declared.

"Do you really think so?" said Chester Steward, and he was serious. "That's our immediate problem. The *Sphere*, you see, wants a Vesta paper to come in with it on the campaign. I've been approached and so has the Colonel. Naturally Upton hasn't because the *Blade* is a Gerard paper and the *Sphere* hates Gerard. But we asked George to this meeting because—well, this looks like a family affair. The public good comes before any paper's interest. We're thinking about the damage to Vesta if the *Sphere* comes out with a national campaign against the Red Riders."

Douglas lit his cigar and smoked. They'd all forgotten me and I wasn't opening my trap. This was too good to miss—inside stuff with the big bosses.

"Why can't the *Sphere* be stopped?" said Douglas after a minute. "I know some very influential men in New York."

Everybody looked a little embarrassed. Whether they were ashamed of Harvey P. Douglas' ignorance or themselves, I don't know.

"I'm afraid that's impossible," said Chester Steward. "If the *Sphere* has decided to go through with this, the *Sphere* will go through with it. That's the *Sphere's* reputation. 'Influence' will do more harm than good. Furthermore, the *Sphere* will offer this exposé to other papers throughout the country. Do you realize what that will mean—half a hundred big newspapers publicizing Vesta as the fountainhead of Jew-baiting, lynch law, race hatred and all the other dirty stuff that's bound to be in this series? Why, it'll take a hundred 'Come-to-Vesta' campaigns to counteract the effect on outside capital and our own industries."

Douglas just sat there.

"God damn," he said. "God damn."

Colonel Cronkhite took his cigar from his mouth. "You see the situation, Harvey. We are asking you as president of the board of trade"—and he lingered over that one—"as president—of the—board of trade—to give us your advice. You say the Red Riders ought to be exposed. I agree with you. But will it do harm or good? And should a Vesta newspaper lend itself to such a scheme? Should either the *Star* or the *Courier* join up with the *Sphere?*"

"Good God no!" said Harvey P. Douglas. "I hope you understand that, boys. Never! And I hope you understand it, too, Mr. Upton. Why, it would be suicide for a Vesta paper to encourage such disloyalty to the city!"

"I shall so report to Mr. Gerard," said Upton. "I will quote your opinion, sir, if I may."

"By all means do," said Douglas. "I know A. B. very well; I am sure he would do nothing to hurt Vesta."

"But," I said, "won't it look awfully funny if Vesta is the only city in the country where not a single paper has the guts to hop the Red Riders?"

I was so interested I honestly hadn't realized I was talking out of turn.

They all looked at me without speaking, except Roberts, who said, "Your opinion wasn't invited, Dudley. Better get along. Any further questions you want to ask him, Colonel?"

"No," said Colonel Cronkhite, and he bowed to me. "Thank you, son." He was always polite to everybody who worked for him, even office boys.

Several of them started talking then and before I got out I heard Colonel Cronkhite say, "I think you are right, Harvey, we should keep out of this. The *Sphere* itself is making a big mistake. The way to kill off those fellows is not by giving them more publicity, but by giving them none. The Red Riders thrive on notoriety. There's more than one way to skin a cat. Now if we keep this exposé out of Vesta—"

All right, I thought, as I closed the door, you may be right, Colonel, but you're missing a swell story—a whale of a story— and if I can help the *New York Sphere* to get it, I'm going to do it. What do I care about Harvey P. Douglas and the board of trade?

CHAPTER SEVEN

BECKWITH ROBINSON, THE STAR REPORTER FOR the *New York Sphere*, had been in Vesta a week before I met him. At that, I met him almost as soon as any newspaper man did. He was leary of the Vesta boys, for he had been warned that their papers wouldn't co-operate and he probably believed all of us were hand in glove with the Red Riders.

He had funny ideas about the South, anyway. Mainly he got them from Mencken before Mencken turned half-Confederate. He believed that all territory below the Potomac was literally a vast desert inhabited by mobs of peasants who roved the land, lynching and burning, under the leadership of Methodist dervishes. He believed no Southerner had ever heard of Beethoven and only one out of a hundred could read and write. He believed the last Southern gentleman died at Shiloh and all Southern ladies were virgins or vampires. He believed the most intelligent people in the South were mulattoes and that, if he met an intelligent white man, he was a mulatto passing as white. He believed a lot more nonsense and the worst of him was, when the reality wasn't precisely what he expected, he got a little angry about it. With his mouth full of the best fried chicken that ever left a griddle, he would denounce Southern cooking fiercely. He seemed to resent anything good he found in the South, and I wondered, sometimes, if what he resented wasn't the discovery that the South could produce an article, whether it was a poem or a football team, the equal of any in the North.

I don't think he was really proud of the North; I think he hated the South for being proud.

Well, Beckwith Robinson had come South to get the lowdown on the Red Riders, and I guess he was a good man for the job. But he must have been surprised, after he had been there a week and finally decided to call on Colonel Cronkhite, by the reception he received. The Colonel, of course, was the soul of cordiality. He asked Robinson to dinner and gave him cards to all the clubs and talked to him for an hour about the *Sphere,* on which the Colonel had been a reporter for two years when he was a young man. On top of that, he brought Robinson up to the city room and introduced him around and told us to do everything we could to help Robinson.

"We don't think much of the Red Riders hereabouts," he said. "We think they're a pretty shoddy outfit for a fine paper like the *Sphere* to be wasting its talent on. Why doesn't the *Sphere* go after those Tammany grafters," he chuckled, "if it's got to expose somebody? But if you're bent on cleaning up our backyard for us, I reckon we should be grateful even if we think you should scour your own kitchen first. Anyhow, you have to get your story, don't you, boy? Dudley, here, can help you. He was Big Boa Constrictor of the Red Riders for a while, I believe."

"This is very nice of you, Colonel," Robinson said. It was about all he could say.

I went to lunch with Robinson. I soon found out that he didn't know much or else he was suspicious. So I opened up, I gave him all the dope I had on the Red Riders, from Rosebud Boggs' cathouse days to Dr. Sloat's caduceus, and when I got through, he not only believed I wasn't lying but he was enthusiastic and grateful.

"Kid," he said, "this story is going to bust the United States wide open. Of course, I already had most of it, and a lot you've told me I can't print. But you've been a big help to me—a big help. If you ever want a job in New York, kid, write me."

I did write him two years later and he never answered, and when I finally went to New York, I could have seen Ochs easier than Beckwith Robinson. But I didn't know back there in Vesta that he was a bastard—I just thought he was an ass. I didn't even mind his calling me "kid"—he was the *New York Sphere* and this was a big story; that was all I cared about.

I didn't see Robinson for two or three days and then he called me up. "H'ar'yu, kid?" he said. "Doing anything tonight?" And when I said no, he asked me to dinner. "I'm a bit fed up with your country clubs and Southern hospitality—this town got any night life? I don't mean society—I'm dirty with society—I mean underworld. The joints, the dumps, the dopes, the hookers, the niggers. Especially the niggers. How's for showing me the darker side of Vesta?"

I said I would fix it and I telephoned a friend of mine, Detective Jeff Broddy, and after drinks and dinner at Robinson's hotel, we put out for police headquarters.

It was Saturday night and Carmine Street was one long, loud, lurid midway. The hotfish stands, the beer saloons and the pool parlors were going full tilt. Every corner had a crowd around a medicine man or a fight. The bells in the auction house were ringing like fire alarms, the Jews yelled from the pawnshop doors, guns banged in the shooting galleries and niggers laughed and surged everywhere. We passed the Dime Museum and the Gospel Mission, we passed the nigger theater showing the Black Follies and a western, we passed the old red light district that the police don't bother any more since the niggers took it over, and we came through more blocks of blaze and sound and niggers to Jeff Broddy and his partner waiting in a Ford car in front of the station-house.

I introduced Robinson as a friend of mine from New York and Jeff said he hoped he wasn't that *New York Sphere* man he'd heard was snooping around.

"Robbie's in the brokerage business," I said. "He's never been South before and he wants to see Darktown. What do you think of it so far, Robbie?"

"A miniature Harlem," said Robinson.

We got in the back of the Ford and started out. Jeff took us to some nigger blind tigers and nigger gambling dens and nigger whore-houses. Everywhere we went the niggers stopped whatever they were doing and bowed and scraped when we came in. "Just lookin' around, boys, just lookin' around," the cops would say, and the niggers would rest easy. We watched a crap game for a while and drank rotgut drinks in two of the blind tigers and saw a hooch dance in a house. The Hole-in-the-Wall was the last place we went. It was a tunnel leading to a backyard where an old woman was tending a charcoal fire. Another nigger was asleep on the ground by the fire and Jeff said they sold cocaine here.

"You don't mean it?" Robinson said. "And just what time do the orgies begin in Vesta?"

"Oh, we'll probably have a few cuttin's and shootin's before mornin'," Jeff Broddy said. "A week ago a nigger cut another nigger's throat from ear to ear in that last crap joint we was in."

Robinson didn't say anything.

"Haven't they got any dance halls?" he wanted to know.

Jeff turned to his partner. "They's a dance down at the Masonic Hall tonight, ain't they, Homer? We might run by there."

We ran by. The dance was being given by the students of Booker T. Washington College. They had Handy's Band from Memphis. The girls wore low-necked dresses and the boys dress-suits, and the dancing was the nicest I'd seen since I went to Professor Pagliotti's as a kid. When I introduced myself and

Mr. Robinson from New York, a mighty polite nigger urged us to come in and have some punch, but we said much obliged, we had to trot along.

"If I'd gone to the country club dance, I'd have got more action for my money," was all Robinson said. But after Jeff and his partner dropped us at Chatauga Avenue, he cut loose.

"Of course, that's about all you can expect, chaperoned by a couple of flatfeet. I knew I should have gone on this Cook's tour alone."

I don't know what he'd counted on—Congo hell, I guess.

"As a matter of fact, if you had," I said, "you'd probably been knocked in the head and rolled. Some of those joints are tough joints."

"Come on!—I know a tough joint when I see one."

"Really they are. They were worse a few years ago, before we had the race riot and the mob went down Carmine Street and tore the white women's pictures out of the dives and killed some mighty bad niggers. The police have Carmine Street pretty well under control now."

"Cowed, you mean. Was that fellow a Red Rider?"

"Jeff Broddy? I guess he is—I dunno."

He thought for a minute and then he said, "Well, it was a very nice little setup, a very nice exhibit to show the inquiring reporter from New York. Congratulate Colonel Cronkhite for me, will you, kid?"

I was pretty sore. After all, it was no treat for me to spend my Saturday night with a lot of bur-heads.

"Look here," I said, "you don't think the colored race in Vesta is any different from the colored race in Harlem, do you? Or much different from the white race, for that matter. Did you expect them to be dancing on the levee or carving each other like hogmeat? Or did you expect to see parties of whites rampaging the streets with ropes and torches? What you saw was the average night in Darktown, the worst and the best of it. But if you're not satisfied," I said, "I'll take you over to the Rainbow and buy you a drink and we'll see if we can't dig you up some rough stuff."

We walked along Manton Avenue, past the closed shops and the Acropolis Hotel and Francetti's, where the soda-jerkers were swabbing down and the waiters piling chairs on tables. It was midnight, when respectable Vesta goes to bed, and in another hour you wouldn't see a soul in the center of town except, perhaps, a trackman in the glare of his blow-torch, the blue sparks shooting up like rockets against the dark sides of office buildings. But at the Rainbow I knew things would be just starting.

We crossed Blakely Square and turned down Shackneau Street and saw the lighted sign ahead.

"Why, that's just a beer saloon," Robinson said. "I've been there."

"You wait," I said.

We went in, passing a dozen men at the bar, and in the back I nodded to Johnny and he pushed the button and we eased through the painted door. The corridor sloped ahead like a runway.

"When you reach the end," I said, "you'll be on Sentinel Street. You'll be in that big house they point out to you as the old home of Governor Brady—the one with the magnolia trees in front and the iron deer and the windows boarded up. There's another entrance like this one on the opposite side. It leads from the Halcyon Hotel. Mike Demarue owns the Halcyon and the Rainbow, and he owns the Brady House. He's a big gambler."

"Well, I'm damned!" said Robinson. "A miniature Chinatown."

The drinking rooms are downstairs in Demarue's place and the gambling rooms upstairs. At least, they were then; I haven't been there in five years. There were rooms for other purposes, too, and if you didn't bring your own girl, the Halcyon had plenty on call. Demarue's was the wickedest spot in Vesta, I suppose, and it certainly was the liveliest—and about the only live spot— at one o'clock in the morning.

Robinson went to the can and I walked on into the bar, which used to be the music room. Demarue had left untouched the murals around the walls depicting Music Through the Ages, except to hang paintings of nudes on top of them and one painting of Custer's Last Fight, but he had changed everything else. Once Adelina Patti had sung here—"The Last Rose of Summer" to a group that included Mrs. President Cleveland; now there was a mirror bar where the grand piano had stood and booths with pink curtains under what was left of Pan and Orpheus and King David. A girl hailed me from one of the booths and I went over and it was Miss Cooper, all ginned up.

"Sit down and talk to me, honey, till my boy friend gets back," she said. "My goodness, I haven't seen you since the old cow died!"

She'd changed, gotten harder, she looked to me like she was on the town. And I was sure she was when I asked her what she was doing these days and she said nothing right now.

Right away she started on George X. Jones, who had fired her from her job, and never in my life have I heard a woman so full of venom. She called him every name you ever saw on a fence and some combinations biologically impossible. According to her, George X. Jones was a dirty soandso who had caused her to quit her home and her family and the fellow she was engaged to, and promised to take her to Washington and New York and Paris, and wanted to marry her, and she would have married him only, thank God! she found out in time what a snake he was and told him so, the dirty little rat, and it was good riddance to him and the job, both, if he thought for a minute she was going to put up with the nasty things he wanted her to do.

"Maybe that little bitch will he's got now, but I wouldn't," she said. "Maybe I'm not pure as snow, but I'm not that kind of a girl. Did you ever see her? You can tell what kind she is, all right, the minute you lay eyes on her. The first day I saw her in the office, 'Yoo hoo!' I said to myself, 'you never grew that face in the nursery,' and that chalky skin and that chalky yellow hair, I said, they ain't the only unnatural thing about you. And the way she looked at men, you could tell it, too, and so could they tell it on her."

Well, I let her rave and when Robinson came in and I called him over and introduced him, I told her to speak freely, he was a pal of mine and a regular fellow.

"Miss Cooper," I said, "was just discussing her old boss who was my boss for a while, George X. Jones. Maybe you've heard of him—he's Supreme Python of the Red Riders."

"Supreme phooey!" Miss Cooper said. "If those Red Riders ever get on to what I know about him, they'll python him."

"You mean his gay philandering?"

She gave me one of those looks. "Don't get me started. I mean his crookedness. You know where he gets that magic water he sells 'em that's supposed to come from some river in India? Right out the tap. It's nothing but plain old Chatauga Phosphate!"

"All our city water," I explained to Robinson, "comes from the Chatauga River."

While I ordered a round of drinks, she told us more about the magic water. Every Lair was required to use magic water at initiations and the Supreme Palace sold it to the Lairs at ten dollars a bottle. Figuring all the Lairs in the country and every new member getting his share of the drops and every bottle bringing nearly a hundred per cent profit, that was a mighty tidy little business.

"Some graft!" I said. "They're getting smart since I left 'em."

"You don't know nothin'," said Miss Cooper. She said the Supreme Palace was selling hoods and robes to the Lairs—at $6.50 per hood-robe. Cost price, $1.25; net per Red Rider, $5.25. She said the Palace sold robes to the Tarantulas and Cobras and the officers of each Lair. She said that Jones had invented all sorts of shields and banners and dinguses for the Lairs; order your dingus from the Supreme Palace. She said he was selling whips advertised as genuine snakeskin and daggers and straps and bugles and caduceuses like Dr. Sloat's. He was even selling Red Rider Bibles because Scripture was used in the "lodge work."

"But where does he get all the stuff?"

"I guess you ain't been out River Road lately. They got a regular factory out there. It's back of the Palace."

"I know," said Robinson. "I went out there, but I couldn't get in."

"Of course you couldn't! They got a high wire fence all around the grounds. It's charged with electricity. They got guards with guns. They'd shoot anybody they caught fooling around."

"And that's where they make the stuff?"

"Not all of it. The Bibles come from some firm in New York and they rip off the covers and put on their own. The daggers and whips and heaps of other things are made up North. Some Jew firm makes them cheap. But they make the robes out there."

"I suppose Mrs. Boggs is in charge of making the robes," I said.

"Don't get me started," said Miss Cooper. "Old sister Boggs is so busy with her own secret society she ain't got time to peek around the block. Not that what she don't know won't hurt her. You know—the Red Circle."

"You mean to say she actually started that thing and the women are joining?"

"Thousands," said Miss Cooper.

"And is she selling the women robes and Bibles and whatnot?"

"I'd like to know what's gonna stop her."

Robinson called the waiter. "I think I want to buy this little girl a drink," he said. "What'll it be?"

"I'll take the same, hon," said Miss Cooper.

She said, "Did you know they were fixing to start a ranch?"

"A ranch?"

"Sure—that's a place they raise horses, ain't it? They're fixing to raise horses and sell 'em to the Lairs. And after that they're fixing to start a whatchucallit."

We waited. "You know," she said, "one of those places they make guns and shells and things. Like in the war—a whatchucallit."

"Munitions factory?"

"That's it—they're fixing to build a munition factory to make guns and cannons for all the Lairs."

"That's hard to believe," said Robinson.

"All right, you don't have to believe it. But I betcha they're a million Red Riders drilling in this country right this minute."

"What for? The war's over."

"What for? They got to keep the foreigners out, ain't they? And they got to be ready to defend the country in case of another war, ain't they? When the time comes, my boy friend says the Red Riders can march into the White House in Washington and run the country like they want. He says they're working on a can-non—like that Big Bertha they had in the war—a cannon that'll stand in the middle of the state of Texas and shoot clean to the Vatican, wherever that is."

"Why not?" I said, winking at Robinson to lay off.

He said, "Is your boy friend a Red Rider?"

Miss Cooper twitched herself and gave me a wink. "Ask me no questions and I'll tell you no lies. He's my little honey man, I'll tell you that much." She began looking around the room. "It's about time that son-of-a-bitch came back," she said.

Robinson asked her some more questions, but she wouldn't answer. She'd let off her steam, I guessed, and wouldn't even rise to the subject of Jones. She said what Robinson didn't know wouldn't hurt him. She said curiosity killed a cat. She said if her boy friend came back and caught her shooting off her mouth, he'd skin her alive. Finally she said, "I've got to powder my nose," and not another drink would keep her.

"She's gone to look for him," I said. "Too bad you asked her if he was a Red Rider. That got her restless."

"Baloney!" said Robinson. "I'd pumped her dry, anyway. Do you believe that fat she was handing us?"

"I believe they're selling the magic water and the other stuff and I wouldn't put it past George X. Jones to start a horse farm or anything else that has jack in it."

"Well, I'd give my shirt to see inside the Supreme Palace," said Robinson.

CHAPTER EIGHT

THE WAY BECKWITH ROBINSON AND I GOT INTO the Supreme Palace was this:

There lived in Vesta, then, a character named Diamond Broyles. He wasn't called that because, like Diamond Jim Brady, he sported diamonds; he was an old baseball player. He had played with Cap Anson's Chicago Colts, he claimed, and after that he had knocked about the world. In the Klondike he had struck it rich and, returning to the States, settled down in Vesta. This was in the bicycle era. Diamond Broyles built a colosseum where Bobby Walthour and other famous riders made their reputations. When the automobile came in, he owned the first car in town. He brought "Diavolo" to Vesta to loop the loop, he started a speedway and organized the first "good roads" tour, he was agent for half a dozen leading cars and he made a lot of money. Everybody knew Diamond Broyles and liked him. And he liked everybody. There wasn't a prominent citizen he didn't hail by his first name and there wasn't a newsboy who couldn't call him "Diamond."

Next to his baseball career, the proudest boast of Diamond Broyles was his hobo days. He had been the friend of A-Number-One, the famous tramp, and after he got rich, A-Number-One used to visit him. He corresponded with other tramps and with Jeff Davis, King of the Hoboes, and once a year he held a Hobo Barbecue on his model truck and dairy farm north of Vesta.

The town, though liking Diamond Broyles, didn't like his Hobo Barbecue. Its fame had spread and from far and wide, when the leaves were turning, hoboes set their faces south to feast on roast pork and Brunswick stew for one day as the guests of Diamond Broyles. Vesta for a week was overrun with hoboes. The board of trade protested, the city council passed stricter vagrancy laws, the railroads and the police cracked down. But Diamond Broyles just laughed. His farm was over the line in Jeptha County, which Diamond Broyles practically owned. He kept on holding the barbecue until the day of his death. The year following, the authorities laid for the hoboes. But not a one showed up in the yards and along the lines where special posses waited for them. Wherever they were, from El Paso to Sitka, the underground news of their friend's death had reached them.

The Vesta newspapers, under civic pressure, had adopted a policy of ignoring the Hobo Barbecue before the event. But on the day it took place we always covered it, and when I drew the assignment that year, I asked Beckwith Robinson to come along. Terry Mason was going out to take pictures and he had room for us in his car.

The morning was fine, golden Indian summer weather that made you think of football and pine-fat fires and scuppernongs ripening in the arbors along the road, and when we got out from the city and began to pass the big homes half hidden by foliage and the hills where sumac already flamed, Beckwith Robinson agreed that the South, for all its drawbacks, was swell country to look at.

We swung around a curve and were going into second on the long hill ahead, when Robinson said, "Isn't that—"

"Yes," I said, " 'Smith's Folly.' Stop a second, Terry."

From the bare crest to our right jutted toward the sky a block of marble and granite that looked as much like a postoffice as it did a castle, and it looked like both. Four white pillars stood out from the pink walls of the first story. Then gray granite began, shooting up two more stories into bastions on the corners and a narrow tower in the center. The sun flashed on something gold at the apex of the tower, and from the bastions flags flew, the Stars and Stripes above one and a red flag of indeterminate design above the other.

On the Rhine or in a great city, the Supreme Palace of the Red Riders might have been both beautiful and sinister, but here, except for a fringe of grass in front and a line of thin new trees across the ridge, there was nothing to become it. An acre of red clay, scarred with gullies and relieved only here and there by patches and threads of broom-sedge, fell away on all sides. Through it, like a strip of tape across a wound, ran a concrete drive, so recently finished that the wooden struts were still in place. Where it ended at the road, half a dozen cars were parked to one side, muddy Fords and hard-driven Buicks. Further on a big scoop dug at the side of the hill and workmen were busy. The entire scene was raw and ugly, and in it the Palace seemed grotesque, became gimcrack and ridiculous, as though it had been dropped there by mistake on the way to a world's fair.

"There she is," said Terry, "Nightgown Hall! If Dudley knows the password, we might drop in and borrow a couple of sheets to scare tramps with."

"You won't get far past that guy at the gate," said Robinson.

A double gate of iron spanned the entrance to the drive, and alongside of us and as far ahead as we could see ran a thick wire fence as tall as the combined height of three tall men. The guardian of the gate wasn't many feet short of the fence. He wore a slouch hat, a sweater and trousers tucked into leather half-boots and I didn't doubt that the holster on his hip held a .45.

As we watched, he began to unloose chains from the gate, and we saw, rolling down the drive from the Palace, a car. It was a heavy, cream-colored limousine of the latest model, but except for the chauffeur, we couldn't tell who was in it. The double gate opened and the car swung to the right and ahead of us into the country. When we reached the top of the hill, it was a smudge of dust a quarter of a mile away.

Crossing into Jeptha County, we picked up a couple of hoboes. They said they had been riding the rods for a week to get to the barbecue. We picked up two more, letting them ride the running-boards, and then we began to pass them regularly, hoboes alone and hoboes in pairs and one company of fifteen, slogging along toward the big sitdown.

The hobo riding next to me was a pale, freckled young fellow who didn't look as old as I was. He wore a cap and a black sateen shirt and a pair of pants tied around the bottoms, to keep out the grit when he was standing on the blinds, he said. Every time he moved he crackled because of the newspapers folded around him inside his clothes. He said his name was the Seattle Kid and he had been on the road since he was thirteen years old and wouldn't swap the life for all of Rockefeller's oil. He said the wanderlust was in his blood—wanderlust was the word he used, too—and he expected to bum his way through every country in the world if the women or the cocaine didn't get him first.

I let him rattle on, hoping he would give me something to make a story. I knew, from having covered them before, that the Hobo Barbecues weren't always as colorful as you'd think. Most of the hoboes were boozy old halfwits who stuffed themselves to the teeth with Diamond Broyles' meat and beer, took a handout and blew with no story more startling than you'd get from a tramp at the back door, or else they were young toughs like this

Seattle Kid who talked about hoboing as if they were actors who had learned a part in a play, and a pretty hackneyed part, too. I've known newspaper reporters like that—they acted the part of Richard Harding Davis if they were only strutting out to cover a luncheon of the Kiwanis Club.

I asked the Seattle Kid if he had ever worked and he said yes, he had worked on construction gangs and in the wheat fields and traveled with a circus, but he hated work because he wanted freedom to follow the call of the wild. He said he was a poet at heart and had written a lot of poems and he would sing me one of them.

> "It was down in the Lehigh Valley [he sang] in early
>   Sixty-three,
> We was panning sand in the Rio Grande, my partner,
>   Bill, and me,
> When Bill got stuck on a gal named Nell, she warn't so
>   goldarn bad—"

I didn't tell him I'd heard "Down in the Lehigh Valley" several hundred times when I was in college. I let him sing it out and "Ring Dang Do" and "Don't look at me that way, stranger" and half a dozen other smutty old ballads he said he wrote. He had a nice tenor voice, anyway.

"What part of the country do you come from originally, Kid?" I asked him, "Seattle?"

He looked at me hard. "That's just my monicker. I got that monicker on account I croaked a punk in Seattle. He'd been a punk to older 'boes for a long time and he wanted me to be his punk and so I croaked him. Where do I hail from? You'd be surprised—I hail from just about fifty miles south of here."

"Margana?"

"Maybe—but I ain't saying. I ain't seen my home town since I was a kiddie. Margana? I had a gal in Margana once, a lovin' little gal named Sue."

I didn't ask him for details, for I figured he was just romancing, and anyway, we were coming into Home Run, which was Diamond Broyles' farm.

You'll go a long way before you'll find a finer farm than Home Run. Acres and acres of pasture and alfalfa and truck gardens, all neat and pretty as a checkerboard, with irrigation ditches and good roads everywhere, with silos and barns and dipping vats and model stables and creameries and butteries and the Lord knows what all. I'm no farmer, so I can't describe it factually, but if you can imagine a nigger's idea of the Land of Canaan, plus everything in a Sears-Roebuck catalogue, you'll have some idea of what Home Run is like.

We could smell that barbecue a half mile away and I don't mean the hoboes. When they throw a barbecue down in our part of the world, they throw it right, and Diamond Broyles had the best barbecue cook alive working for him, a nigger named Poke Kingsmountain. Yes, sir, that was his name, Poke Kingsmountain. He was famous all over the country. Folks would send for him from as far away as New Orleans and Richmond to superintend a barbecue. He had cooked barbecues for society people in Palm Beach and for national political conventions and for opera stars in Atlanta and big sports at the Kentucky Derby. When Diamond Broyles gave a barbecue, Poke Kingsmountain laid himself out. He would start fatting those shotes months ahead and for a week before the 'cue he would have a hundred niggers in training for it like chorus girls for a Broadway show.

When we came in sight of the barbecue grounds, they were already covered with people and more kept arriving by car and afoot every minute, until, by noon, there must have been five hundred, as many of them friends of Diamond Broyles as they were hoboes. You had to be careful, Diamond Broyles being the kind of host he was, not to mistake an honest citizen of Jeptha County for Panhandle Pete.

The grounds were about a whoop and a holler, as they say in the country, from the main farm buildings. They were around a grove of oak trees on a knoll. The deep woods were not far beyond, but the pits, of course, were in the open field. Here, as long as a long furrow, a trench had been dug exactly deep enough and wide enough for the meat to swing across it over hot coals. That fire had been built of small pieces of green oak and hickory, and maybe ten trees had been cut down to feed it. At sundown the night before the fire had been lit and the meat hung, and all night long niggers had sweated there, basting the meat with long mops dipped in warm salt water tinctured with cayenne pepper. Sometime before, Poke Kingsmountain had personally butchered between twenty and thirty fifty-pound pigs, hacking off the heads and feet, slicing each pig longitudinally down the backbone, running long iron spits through the hams and shoulders and strapping with haywire shorter irons through the sides of the carcass—this to keep the cooking meat from dropping into the fire. The heads and feet, and the livers and hearts, he had saved. They would go into iron kettles with okra and tomatoes and fine-chopped corn and sweet peppers and juices out of Poke Kingsmountain's own bottles, which he would never tell anybody what they contained. This was the Brunswick stew. In another pot he had mixed the barbecue sauce, vinegar and mustard and onions and only God and Poke Kingsmountain knew what. Then Poke Kingsmountain had stayed up with his niggers, coaxing them and cussing them to keep turning and basting, and along toward dawn with his own hands he had basted the pigs with the barbecue sauce, and soon after that the first hobo had come loping over the hill, his eyes on a film of wood-smoke and his nose down on the trail of a scent like no mulligan's on earth.

The result of all that munificence and labor and care was victuals that you might have laid before a Roman emperor instead of a regiment of hoboes. But I guess Diamond Broyles didn't care so long as his guests fetched along their appetites. He had no cause for complaint there. The hoboes and the citizens were bearing down on that barbecue like horses on the hay-box—a hobo with a hunk of spare-ribs in one fist and a mess of Brunswick stew in the other, and right next to him a citizen with both hands full and gravy dripping over his whiskers till you couldn't tell which was hobo and which was citizen.

You don't use knives and forks at a barbecue unless you are a tenderfoot; maybe a wooden spoon, though a heel of bread is better for pushing and sopping. You just tear into it two-handed and bare-handed. And don't think pork and stew was the entire menu. There were sides of barbecued beef and hillocks of cold slaw and mountains of light bread and rye bread and corn bread and cold biscuits. There were roasting ears hot from the ashes and trays of melted butter to pour on them. There were roasted yams and sweet pickles and sour pickles and pickled peaches and preserved quinces and scuppernong jelly and muscadine jelly and sandwiches made out of them. There was sponge cake and chocolate cake and angel cake and devil cake and cherry pie and mince pie and sweet potato pie. There was hot coffee and cold beer. There was persimmon beer and Coca-Cola. You got the beer from a line of kegs at the edge of the woods, you went to the tables in the grove for pie and cake and bread and sandwiches and salad, you called at the bonfire for roasting ears and yams, you circled back to the pits for another helping of barbecue and stew, but mostly you just loafed around in the mild sunshine, sopping it up and sopping up the food and not saying much of anything to anybody.

About twelve o'clock I went to the house and telephoned a story to the paper and on my way back to the barbecue I passed a bunch of cars I hadn't seen before. One of them was the cream-colored car we had noticed coming out of the Supreme Palace of the Red Riders. But I didn't spot Dr. Sloat until the middle of the afternoon and then I heard him first.

The barbecue was beginning to break up. Some of the citizens were driving away and some of the hoboes were catching rides. The hoboes were full to the neck, but every one of them toted his handout in a handkerchief or a can or a sack. They could have swiped whole pies if they'd wanted to, and I guess some of them did, but the majority took pork and stew. About half were still eating—I watched one big tramp eat steady for an hour and forty minutes—and not a few had gone to sleep in fence corners and in the woods. The singing came from the woods, near the farthest beer keg. When I heard it, I hunted up Beckwith Robinson. "If you want to meet the Supreme Serpent of the Red Riders," I said, "come on."

They were singing "Down by the old mill stream" when we strolled up, Dr. Sloat and Gabe Trippy and a third fellow, singing with their heads together and their arms around each other in a little clearing where a spring ran out from under a rock. The third fellow was the Seattle Kid. There was a fourth fellow sitting on his hams by the spring. He had a jug. He wasn't singing, but every time they finished a barbershop chord, he would pour from the jug into a tin dipper and hand it up and they would swap the dipper around. It was peach brandy, white, and about two hundred proof.

Dr. Sloat was mightily pleased to see me.

"Son," he said, "you're a sight for Sunday, you're as welcome as the flowers in May. Sit you down! Sit you down and have a small libation with us. We cannot offer you mead and ambrosia, but here in Nature's own cathedral, from this rude vessel, you may imbibe a native nectar not without virtue. Ganymede," he said to the fellow on the ground, who had only one eye and a blue scar like a lizard running from the lid of the other into his shirt collar, "pour!"

Robinson and I drank from the dipper and passed it, and I introduced Robbie and told the Doc he was looking fine. He was, too, for all he was nobly drunk—shaved to the pink and diked out in broadcloth and a frilled shirt and a skyblue vest with a watch-chain across it like the chains on the Supreme Palace. He wore his planter's hat and he carried the umbrella case which I knew held his caduceus.

The Doc was in fine form.

"We are celebrating this delightful occasion," he said, "with song. I am sure my good friend, Diamond Broyles, would not object should we troll another measure. Gentlemen, what shall it be—When You and I Were Young, Maggie,' or 'Silver Threads Among the Gold'?"

The Seattle Kid, who seemed to be holding his liquor like a major, said, "I got a good one—wrote it myself—she goes like this." And he started—

"Oh, I met Miss Malone in the graveyard—"

But he hadn't sung the first verse when the Doc stopped him.

"Son, son, let us not profane this pastoral scene, let us not sully the fair name of womanhood. Besides, I knew a Miss Malone once—a sterling soul, the queen of her sex—she was not at all like the lady you describe."

The Seattle Kid looked resentful, but since he didn't know whether Sloat was a bishop or the sheriff, he shut up. The Doc put his arm around him and apologized.

"Forgive an old man's eccentricities, my boy—song is sacred to me. Song is the manna in life's wilderness, the attribute of the angels, the hallmark of eternal motherhood. And you, my boy, have an angel's voice; it reminds me of my own dear mother's. Gabe, how about a hymn?"

Reverend Trippy led off with the hymns. Every time he started a new one, he hummed it first and the Doc taught the Seattle Kid the words. When they reached "Revive Us Again," we all joined in. Robinson turned out to have a fair baritone and I'm not a bad second tenor myself. Ganymede didn't sing—he grinned and said nothing—but he was right there with the dipper after every hymn.

We sang a lot of hymns. We finished the peach brandy. Sometime during the afternoon, I remember, Terry Mason was there, saying something about leaving. We told him we'd go in a minute. Sometime later a big guy in a corduroy vest was telling us we had to go. He really was the sheriff. I remember the Doc gave him an argument. I remember Ganymede telling the Doc to hush. I remember thinking at the time, "Gosh, for a hobo that bird is certainly rough with the Supreme Serpent of the Red Riders."

"Very well, suh," the Doc told the sheriff, "we shall go where the music of the church is more warmly appreciated and more comfortably rendered. I am surprised at my old friend, Diamond Broyles."

I remember his saying that and I remember getting in the car. But I didn't know whose car it was or that Sloat, Trippy, Ganymede, Robinson and the Seattle Kid all got in, too. For, to be frank about it, I went to sleep as soon as I hit the cushions.

The rattle of chains woke me—and Robinson punching me in the side. "Wake up, kid," he was whispering, "wake up—this is it." We were in a glare like a battleship's beam. I couldn't see a thing as the car rolled gently ahead. Then it went up a slope and out of the searchlight's path and though it was dark, I could see better—a pair of pillars, a flight of wide stone steps and at the top of them, light.

I wish I could describe the Supreme Palace of the Red Riders as we saw it, but you'll have to go to a better reporter than I was that night. Beckwith Robinson did a good job in the columns of the *New York Sphere*—the great hall, the vaulted roof with its cut-glass chandelier, the banners and strange insignia on the walls, the floor of tiles patterned in the image of a huge red cobra, and the time-clock, the benches, the lettered glass doors and the other everyday traps of business. "It was," Robinson wrote, "a cross between Potash and Perlmutter and a Hollywood movie set."

Apparently we arrived before the six o'clock whistle blew, for lights were on everywhere, typewriters clicked behind the doors and a number of people were about, looking not at all like Red Riders. Dr. Sloat led the way, his arm around the Seattle Kid, Ganymede helping him on the other side. We crossed the hall, descended iron steps, Ganymede unlocked a door with a key he took from his pocket and it didn't need Sherlock Holmes to figure out that we were in the grand crypt.

If the scene-painters for the Chamber of Horrors, Way Down East and Ten Nights in a Barroom had decided to throw in together, they would have achieved something like this. Baleful were the red walls and black ceiling covered with writhing snakes, weird was the golden throne under a black canopy and the skull on a pulpit and the globe above them that shone like a bloody moon when the Doc turned a switch. But when he switched her again and the room came white and you saw a spittoon and a sofa and a rocking chair, and when he pulled a curtain and revealed a little red organ, and pulled another and out rolled a baby's perambulator full of bottles, and when Ganymede rustled chairs and the Doc said, "Rest yourselves, gentlemen, the bathroom is right back there"—well, you couldn't believe you were in the arcanum of the American mafia.

The Doc cracked out whiskey and glasses, Reverend Trippy sounded a come-all-ye on the organ and Ganymede rooted around the throne and came up with a banjo. Everything looked set for old home week, when a bell rang somewhere in the crypt.

"Who in Sam Hill's that?" said the Doc. He yelled out, "Cum clab ad Clastra!" and the old devil winked at me when he did it.

"They cain't h'yar you from in h'yar, Sim," said Ganymede. That drawl never came from north of the Chatauga Valley; it was a cinch by this time that he was no hobo but a sort of wet-nurse to Sloat.

The bell rang again and the Doc mumbled a few cusses and went weaving to the door. He unbolted it and we heard him say, "Good evening, my dear." Whoever his dear was, she talked too low for the rest of us to understand her. Suddenly the Doc said, loud and sputtery, "Present my compliments to Mrs. Boggs and tell her I'll see who I durn please!" He slammed the door, shot the bolt and came weaving back to us shaking his wattles like a turkeycock.

"An admirable woman, Mrs. Boggs—the queen of her sex—but trying sometimes, gentlemen, very trying. Gimme a shot, Buck, and by gad, gentlemen, if you want to shuck down your galluses and take off your shoes, go to it!"

Ganymede (Buck by rights, I judged) poured out the drinks chuckling like a fool. His grin broke that blue scar like one knife cut across another.

"You cain't whup her, Sim, you know you cain't whup her if she gits her back up," he said.

Sloat let go a noise half snort and half grunt and we all took our glasses.

"To the ladies, God bless 'em!" he said. We hadn't drunk the toast when the bell rang again.

This time it was Vasco. He came in without asking, past the Doc's protesting hand, and he stood looking at us with a professional tough guy's squint when he knows he's in his home alley. He passed up Trippy at the organ and Buck, hunkered on the floor with the banjo across his knees. He passed me up, after staring at me hard, because I guess he remembered seeing me before and thought I belonged. Maybe he passed up Robinson for the same reason. Anyway, the guy he picked was the Seattle Kid.

"You fella," he said, jerking his thumb over his shoulder, "outside!"

The Seattle Kid got up. He looked uncertain but surly, as if he'd been bounced out of worse places than this.

"Whatsa devil's big idea?" the Doc broke in. He was powerful drunk.

Vasco just squinted at him.

"Those man spy," he said, pointing at the Seattle Kid. "He is spy for newspaper. Mrs. Boggs say—poosh him out."

Robinson and I didn't look at each other. I might have felt less than flattered if I hadn't begun to feel mighty uncomfortable. But the Doc wasn't taking anything off Vasco.

"I don't care who he is, you get outa here!" he yelped, and he seized Vasco by the coat.

Vasco brushed him off as if he'd been a bad child. It was kind of pitiful—the old man staggered, he sat down on the sofa and he couldn't get up.

"Outside, you fella," said Vasco.

The Seattle Kid—honestly scared now, I believe—took a step back and Vasco took a step forward and then Buck or Ganymede or whatever his name was, rose between them in one easy stretch. He was a head taller than Vasco and not half his weight, so that he stooped over him like a beanpole over a barrel, but for all his scrawniness there was the same crouch about him that there is in a mean cat and, with that banjo hooked over one arm, he made you think of mountaineers ready for the revenooers in Bloody Breathitt. For a second I had a wild flashback to Doc Sloat's sword-cane and the notion that a banjo could hold a sawed-off shotgun as well as not.

"Leave him be, mister."

Vasco pulled up short.

Buck said, slow as sorghum, "I ain't got but one eye, mister, since a feller hoed the yuther out with his thumb one night whilst we was rasslin'. You got two good 'uns. I'd be mighty proud and happy to git me a eye. Sim—thar—say the word, you and me go to rasslin'."

Vasco, Buck, the Seattle Kid—the three of them didn't move. I don't know how Robinson felt, but I had my spot picked out behind the organ.

Nothing happened because the door, which Vasco must have left half shut, opened wide with a bang and Mrs. Boggs sailed in like a head-nurse into a hospital. She looked exactly that, too—in a white uniform up to her chin, with a thing half cap and half crown on her head, with her pincenez high on her nose and smiling one of those phony smiles a woman does when she could eat her young. Behind her I saw a tall thin girl with a lot of blonde hair, but it didn't strike me then that she was George X. Jones' girl, the one Kitty Cooper was giving hell that night.

"How do you do, Mr. Dudley?" said Mrs. Boggs, pulling up near the Doc on the sofa. "We would be so happy to see you some other time—and your friend from the *New York Sphere!* Come around next week—won't you—when Mr. Jones returns. I'm sure he'll be delighted! But not tonight—we're not at home tonight—the Doctor isn't home tonight, are you, Doctor?"—she whirled on him like a hen on a worm—"You poor old petty! You sweet, tired, self-sacrifighting old dear!"—with every word she scuffled his head till you wondered he had a hair left—"bringing guests home with you, entertaining them when you must be all tuckered out!" She whirled back at us. "He's such an old petty, always doing something for others and him with stomach ulsters so bad he ought to be flat on his back in the bed."

The Doc groaned—he did, indeed, sound sick.

Up to this moment I don't believe Mrs. Boggs, being as flustered as she was, had taken a good look at anybody in the room outside me and the Doc. Now she turned on Robinson.

"Is this the gentleman from the *Sphere?*"

Robbie was about to answer when Vasco made some sort of gesture and the Seattle Kid moved and Mrs. Boggs flashed a look his way. The result astonished all of us. Her eyes popped, her mouth opened, she uttered one yell—"Henery!"

And by golly, it was Henery.

"Hi, maw," he said. He was the real McCoy.

CHAPTER NINE

WE QUIT THE SUPREME PALACE THAT NIGHT CONsiderably cockeyed, both from liquor and what we had seen. We quit it like a couple of visiting Cobras, with salaams from all, and we were driven back to Vesta in state, in the cream-colored limousine, by a uniformed chauffeur as polite as he was tight-mouthed. We were excited, astonished, amused and curious as well as fuddled, but I can't say we knew a lot more about the Order of Red Riders than we did before Diamond Broyles' barbecue.

Behind us we left a scene that, if it had been a barroom, you would have thought, "What godawful drunks!" or, if it had been the house next door, you probably would have called the cops to stop the noise, but, because it was the grand crypt of a national secret society with more than a million members, made you wonder, "Can this be America?"

Mrs. Boggs on the sofa, sunk in tears and whiskey. Henry, the Seattle Kid, taking her slobber without a peep except to crackle now and then when she hugged him. He had become practically comatose; I imagine he woke next morning the most bewildered hobo in sixteen states. But, being a youth who knew a fatted calf when he saw it, I guess he didn't take long to forget the call of the wild and play the prodigal son .... At the organ Gabe Trippy and Dr. Sloat trying to sing, and Buck trying to play on the banjo, "In this weary world there's no other, and God gives you only one mother!" ... Vasco, the bird on every party who won't drink and won't go, glowering from a corner at Buck one minute and

Henry the next. Miss Gobbett doing her stuff as the hostess's best girl friend after the hostess has passed out …. That was the way I remember them and the picture can't be far wrong.

This Miss Gobbett rates a look in any account of the Red Riders, and she may as well get it here. Wanda Gobbett—the Elsie books gone hussy. Wanda, the smart little, ugly little girl of your schooldays—the one who was always whispering to other little girls and told the teacher the time Willie Thompson yelled the bad word—Wanda, who was going to be a missionary to the South Seas but turned up years later as the siren in that church scandal where the minister had to resign—Wanda Gobbett, still offensively pert, still horsefaced and frigid-looking, but with a skittish horse's switch to her hips and the gleam of a mean mare in her eye as she crossed the room.

"Hello, Frank Dudley," she said to me, "don't you know me?" and I didn't for a minute and when she said, "I'm Wanda Gobbett," all I could think to say was, "Good Lord, what are you doing here?"

"I'm Mr. Jones' secretary"—even then I didn't place her as the girl Kitty Cooper called a bitch.

"Where is Mr. Jones tonight?" I said.

"Oh, he's out of town"—she gave me that look of suspicion and superiority she used to flash around a classroom before she showed up the other kids with the right answer—"but when he's away, I look out for things for him." She might as well have added, "And don't think he won't hear about *this* business!"

I tumbled then. I thought to myself, goodnight! is Jones chasing this sourball? And then I remembered Celia, the red-headed dish-washer, and I didn't doubt he'd chase anything. I hope he catches her, I thought to myself. For she was that kind of woman; if she'd been criminally assaulted, you'd have enjoyed hearing of the outrage.

All this was after the Seattle Kid was discovered to be Henry Boggs—after Mrs. Boggs had cried over him and laughed over him and we had another drink and toasted her and toasted him and toasted them both together and everybody had all but forgotten spies were present. Mrs. Boggs had to get his whole story out of Henry, from the time he ran away from home to his descent on the barbecue, and then she had to tell us about Henry's childhood and what a cute baby he was and how, if he had his rights, he would be one of the richest young men in the state and, "yes, sir," she said, "he will be, if he'll promise never to leave his poor mamma again!" and with that she broke down and bawled. She said she was going to give Henry a thousand dollars as a coming-home present, and she did then and there, sending Miss Gobbett to the auditing crypt for it, and Henry broke down and bawled and I guess it was about that time that Doc Sloat and Trippy started their mother songs.

Me, I was ready to sing with them and so was Beckwith Robinson, who, if I'm any judge, had clean forgotten he was a reporter for the *New York Sphere.* But Vasco didn't forget and neither did Wanda Gobbett, and before we knew quite how it happened, we were on our way in the Supreme Serpent's car.

The next day, when I met Robinson, I was pretty sore and blue. It looked to me as if we'd missed a swell chance to get more lowdown on the Red Riders and I was ashamed of myself for blowing it for a cheap drunk. But Robbie was chipper as a partridge. He said his invasion of the Palace was all he needed to complete his investigation. He said his "trap" for Dr. Sloat and Mrs. Boggs was a master-stroke and he was glad Jones hadn't been there to spoil it. He said Sloat had revealed himself as the country's wiliest and wickedest demagogue since Aaron Burr. He said Mrs. Boggs was a second Madam DuBarry and the "other conspirators"—by whom I suppose he meant Vasco, Miss Gobbett, Buck and Trippy—were all in a plot to overthrow democratic government and establish an empire of Anglo-Saxon white Protestant supremacy which they would rule like lords.

"Kid," he said, "when I tell 'em at the *Sphere* how I tricked those devils into dining and wining me in the Palace itself, they'll admit it was the greatest piece of reporting since St. Luke covered the crucifixion!"

I stared at him hard, wondering how drunk I'd been, and I give you my word I almost believed him myself, he was that convincing. But for the sake of the record and to understand some of the events that happened later, let's see how far Robinson was right in laying such ambitions and sinister motives to the ringleaders of the O-R-R.

If you ask me, I believe the simple itch for money was the motive of them all. George X. Jones, from the first, worked the O-R-R for money as brazenly as a pitchman at a circus works the peas. Mrs. Boggs, being a woman and practical minded, didn't have to be told that money makes the mare go. Dr. Sloat may have been a messiah, a drunkard, a demagogue and a clown, but I have seen him at his bleariest stuff a dollar bill in his sock and I cannot believe that anything greater or less than greed for money swayed him when more than the price of a drink was at stake.

There was so much money! At one time the Supreme Treasury was said to be receiving thirty-five thousand dollars a day and, during the years the Red Riders were riding their highest and widest, a total of sixty millions is known to have gone into their coffers. No wonder those nearest to all that loot coveted it; no wonder they sat around the Supreme Palace like so many strange dogs around a bone! Look at them—

Dr. Sloat resented bossing and suspected Jones and Mrs. Boggs of scheming to undermine him and overthrow him, which they probably were.

Jones despised Sloat, but he feared and distrusted Mrs. Boggs. Mrs. Boggs despised and distrusted Jones and Sloat both.

Sloat had Trippy on his side and Buck, who probably was the only one in the outfit who didn't care a damn for money.

Jones had Wanda Gobbett, working for him and working him.

In Mrs. Boggs' corner was Vasco, the bull she had bought. He double-crossed her while he spied for her. And now she had Henry to spy on Vasco.

How many other sweethearts and pimps, sycophants and squealers, strong-arm boys, gunmen, ex-preachers and commission-men there were, lying and loving and scrapping and knifing to get at the cash, I don't know. There must have been plenty, and pretty soon there would be the King Cobras of forty Dens, coming down like the Assyrian, like the wolf on the fold. And all after money!

Yet whatever treacheries and hatreds perforated the Supreme Palace, there they unmistakably were, the three who so short a while before had been a drunkard, a cheap crook and a slut in the backwash of a second-rate city, now a trinity whom a great newspaper could seriously accuse of menacing the peace and government of the United States. If it sounds fantastic, please remember that at the moment the *New York Sphere* was training its searchlight on the "masked menace" below the Potomac, Washington already was a rotten apple of graft, debauchery and high crime touching the honor and the very life of the President himself. The Ohio gang got to the White House before the Red Riders got a good start. And that was about the only difference except, in the case of one set of crooks, nobody, not even the Democratic and crusading *Sphere,* yelled "Wolf!" until the safe was cracked.

Well, the Harding scandals are no part of this story. Beckwith Robinson returned to New York, the weeks passed, President

Harding golfed at Piping Rock, President Harding reviewed the cadets at West Point, President Harding spoke for world peace, President Harding went fishing; then, on a morning when subway readers of other New York papers flipped past the front page to more interesting departments, the *Sphere* began its exposé of the O-R-R.

I have been in New York City, at a later day, when for weeks its papers screamed about Germany's persecution of the Jews and I have wondered, as I heard New Yorkers talk, if they realized the apathy of wide stretches of the hinterland on topics that deeply stir them. Likewise, mentioning Hitler to a Kansan or a Georgian, I have wondered if they had the remotest idea of how intensely several millions of their fellow countrymen in New York feel on this matter. The gulf is not worth noting but for its bearing on public reception of the *Sphere's* crusade.

The *Sphere* did a good job, thorough, accurate, uncompromising, from the record of Dr. Sloat's arrest for petty larceny in 1915—an incident involving two niggers and a mule which loyal Red Riders at the Vesta courthouse had forgotten to hide from the curious Mr. Robinson—to printing columns of Red Rider hocus-pocus, including the "secret oath" and the form for membership application. The series ran for weeks. In retrospect it seems a little solemn, a little hysterical, but perhaps that was the successful way to present it to a people who had lately swallowed the Red Scare whole and who, a few years before, had believed every Hun bayonet was bright with the gore of Belgian infants.

I can imagine, on that morning the subway readers gulped the *Sphere's* headlines and went on to details of floggings and brandings, of hooded horsemen and fiery serpents, of Dread Scorpions and Terrible Tarantulas, of an invisible power creeping by night into their neighborhoods and their homes, I can imagine how they read with genuine concern and looked with awe and repulsion on the foolish photo of Dr. Sloat in his robes, and I can imagine, if they were of a race or faith so unmistakably proclaimed as the foe and prey of those implacable "one hundred per cent Americans," how their concern changed to fear and their repulsion to fury.

It was not surprising that, in New York, the *Sphere's* circulation boomed, that it sold out every edition day after day, that other New York papers were forced to take up the hue and cry, that the Mayor of New York officially proclaimed the Red Riders outlawed, that Red Rider parades in New Jersey and on Long Island were broken up with riot and bloodshed and that, before long, priests and rabbis were addressing mass-meetings and Congressmen were receiving petitions of protest and the President was urged to stamp out the Red Riders as he would the boll weevil.

It was not surprising that in Chicago, in Boston, in every large city with Catholic, Jewish and Negro populations of any consequence, the same tumult rose, for, as our Vesta editors had predicted and feared, the *Sphere's* exposé was syndicated to more than fifty other newspapers and everywhere our vaunted "comet city" was reviled by her sisters for the thing she had spawned. But neither is it surprising that not alone in Vesta but in most of the sister cities—in New York itself, for that matter—reaction was not always indignant. Some read with indifference, some with amusement and many, to speak the plain truth, with hot sympathy for the O-R-R. It is not so that all Americans think alike because they buy the same brand of razor blades and drive Ford cars.

Hence, approaching the Supreme Palace a few days after the *Sphere's* first blast, I did not find it a sinking ship or a beleaguered fortress but in a state bordering on exultation. I had come in the course of duty to get one of those disclaimers from the Supreme

Serpent and, as usual, wound up in the crypt of propagation opposite the Imperial Python.

Prosperity had put flesh on George X. Jones since I last saw him, and a wardrobe fit for a duke. Fawn spats choked the ankles slung across his desk, his chest thrust out a monogrammed shirt and a royal purple tie, he opened a box of Corona-Corona cigars and, when he talked, diamonds flashed from his fingers. Only the scruffy red eyebrows and the broken teeth belonged to the George X. Jones of old. Today he was in fine feather.

What about the attack by the *New York Sphere?*

Lies, all lies. The *Sphere* had fallen for a lot of fake stories invented by irresponsible and disgruntled parties ... the so-called "ritual" was a complete fabrication ... the "secret oath" a mendacious joke ....

But how can that be when, according to the *Sphere,* the ritual and oath are on file in the copyright office in Washington?

Oh, *that* ritual! *that* oath! Of course, the O-R-R had to file something in Washington, but the real secrets of the Order were known only to the initiate, to thirty-second degree Red Riders ....

Thirty-second degree Red Riders?

"Sure!" said George X. Jones. "You don't think every hick that joins attains full brotherhood right off the bat, do you? It takes time—and money!—to cross the seven fiery seas. For instance, the boys that crave action, that want a little of the rough stuff— but I'm not talking for publication now, Dudley, we never countenance violence"—and he smirked.

Then you disclaim responsibility for all those outrages the *Sphere* reports?

That's right. Committed by thugs and vandals masquerading as Red Riders. The O-R-R is as upright and decent as the Masons or the Elks or, as far as that goes, the Knights of Columbus. Why doesn't the *Sphere* attack them? Protestants have as much right to organize as Jews and Catholics. The O-R-R is simply a patriotic, philanthropic, eleemosynary—

I know, I know. Let's skip that. What about those quotations the *Sphere* ran from the *Cyclops?* They don't sound very philanthropic and eleemosynary toward the Jews and Catholics.

Very exaggerated. Cut and garbled .... Of course, our motto is, "First for America and for Americans first—"

I know. Let's skip that, too .... What about the *Sphere's* charge that the O-R-R is going in for politics and hopes to elect the governors and legislatures of several states?

Jones grinned. "Why not? To be fair with you, I hadn't thought about it before, but the suggestion's good. Thank the *Sphere* for me."

"You don't seem very worried by the *Sphere's* attack."

"Worried? Why, look here"—and he picked up a pile of letters—"know what these are? New applications for membership in the Red Riders. Know where they came from? Mostly New York and New Jersey. Know where they got the application blanks? Cut 'em out of the *New York Sphere!*"

He threw back his head and cackled.

"No, sir! The *New York Sphere's* 'crusade' is the greatest thing that ever happened to the Red Riders. Nation-wide publicity! And, believe me, we're going to cash in on it one hundred per cent. We'll double our membership in a month. I predict five million Red Riders in this country by Christmas. The first of the year we'll be holding a Grand Reptilon in Vesta that'll beat any convention this town ever saw. You mark my words."

"That all you got to say?" I asked him. "What about the *Sphere's* story that you're a swindler and the Doc stole a mule once and Mrs. Boggs used to run a cat-house?"

He looked at me as if I'd gone crazy.

"All I've got to say? Boy, I've just started! We'll get down to brass tacks now." He pushed a button on his desk. Wanda Gobbett came in. She didn't look at me. "Miss Gobbett, take this for the reporters. Dr. Simeon D. Sloat, Supreme Serpent of the Veiled Legion of the Right Royal and Venerable Order of Red Riders, today gave out the following statement from the Supreme Palace, quotes:

"I have instructed our attorneys in New York City to file suit immediately against the *New York Sphere* for one hundred thousand dollars damages for libelous statements contained in the vicious series of articles being published by that newspaper. Our Order has likewise engaged counsel in every State in the Union to file similar suits against any and all newspapers that have published or may publish the *Sphere's* libelous attack. End quotes."

"Dr. Sloat said, quotes, this base and venemous plot—"

He dictated slush for ten minutes and though I knew he was bluffing and he knew I knew it, I had to hand it to him for beautiful buncombe before he wound up, "That's all, sweetheart—I guess that'll sound pretty good to the boys back in South Bend!"

Of course, those suits never were filed. The *Sphere* kept right on publishing its exposé and Jones kept right on giving out statements. In New York and Chicago the boys kept on breaking up Red Rider parades and yelling for a Congressional investigation, and in Indiana and Texas the boys kept on beating up chumps and yelling for one hundred per cent America. If it wasn't for the chumps, you could be right cynical—you could say the big crusade did everybody a lot of good, including the *Sphere* and the O-R-R.

But to be honest about it, I don't agree with those who hold that the *New York Sphere* was the making of the Red Riders, who say—and some say it yet—that if it hadn't been for the *Sphere*, the O-R-R would have been laughed to death or expired of its own tomfoolishness. For one American who deserted the O-R-R because the *Sphere* shamed him out of it, there were probably ten who joined because they read in the *Sphere* how sinister and exciting it was. That much is true. And as for killing the O-R-R by government decree, the Congressional investigation, which was finally held, got about as far as you would expect a Congressional investigation to get. They say, when the mysterious Supreme Serpent was summoned to testify, Jones used a ringer and that "Golden Gabe," subbing for the pie-eyed Doc as he had at many a Reptilon, had those Senators hog-tied. In any event, too many Congressmen heard from the wool-hat boys back home to make a vote against the O-R-R popular.

The *Sphere's* big accomplishment never showed on the surface. I doubt that its editors realize to this day the smartest thing they did. They printed the box-office returns .... One sucker, $10. Cut to Cobra, $4. Cut to Tarantula, $1. Cut to Supreme Treasury, $5. One bottle magic water, $10. One hood-robe, $6.50 .... There, brothers, was the fuse that blew the keg.

It started sizzling one cold night in early December when the *Sphere's* exposé was all over but the mumbling. My telephone at home rang and it was Joe Deadwyler.

"Get a car and go out to River Road," he said. "They've just called me from police. Mrs. Rosebud Boggs' house. She's been assassinated."

Everybody knew where Mrs. Boggs lived. It was the old Dooley Hinman place. When Dooley Hinman died at eighty-six as stingy as he was rich, his young widow beat it to Paris by the fastest boat and cabled the executors to sell everything. The first bidder on Roselands, famous gardens and all, was Mrs. Rosebud Boggs, newly swollen by Red Rider gold. She got it. Her neighbor on the east was Henderson Tyne, life-president of the Vesta Riding and Driving Club, and on the west Mrs. Albert Sidney

Johnston Green, historian of the Daughters of the Confederacy, but though they never spoke to Mrs. Boggs and fought the sale in court and frequently called the cops when she was throwing parties for visiting Cobras, she held on to Roselands. I think she was stuck on the name and probably told the Cobras her dear, dead mother christened her for the family estate.

I got Joe Deadwyler's telephone call a little before eleven o'clock, it took the Spider Agency half an hour to send a taxi, and we were another thirty minutes, going fifty to sixty, before we hit the River Road. So it was past midnight when we reached Roselands. Even so, the police weren't two minutes ahead of us and that—which I'll come back to later—was one of the queerest things about that very queer evening.

The night was the soft, bright, eerie kind winter often brings to the far south, when the moon is clear as crystal overhead and you feel rather than see a haze everywhere. I saw the tail-light of the police car as if it was a long way off and then suddenly it disappeared and we had run past the Boggs place before we knew it. When we turned around we still hadn't come to the Greens' gate and I remember thinking, "Shucks, her parties couldn't have bothered the neighbors much, that far away."

I suppose I was feeling sorry for the old girl, lying dead in her own blood, and I can tell you it was a shock when, as we were trundling up the drive, the first thing I heard was the voice of Mrs. Boggs, coming out strong from the illuminated house into all that hush and moonlight. She was weeping, to put it politely, and calling for Henry. My driver killed his engine and I got out and I heard Henry answer back, "Yes, Maw, yes!"

Henry was in the front hall, talking to the police. There were two officers and a third man, Pete Barron, a reporter for the *Morning Star*. He looked chagrined when I walked in.

"How did you get here so quick?"

"My office 'phoned me."

"My office 'phoned me," he said. "I was at police. The cops didn't know anything about it."

We didn't stop then to figure that out, for Henry was leading the way and we followed. At the north end of the big living-room was a bay window with a lounge under it and a lamp on a table. The windowpane had been smashed to hell. There was glass all over the lounge and all over the floor. There were two bullet holes in the lampshade.

"She was sittin' right there," said Henry, "read-in' a book, when about ten or 'leven o'clock the shots came, bang, bang! They musta knocked out the light 'cause when I run in every-thing was dark and I could just see her in the light from the other room. I yelled 'Maw!' and run over and there she was unconscious and all covered with blood! I thought sure she was dead."

"Wounded?" said a cop.

"Naw," said Henry, "just cut."

Mrs. Boggs began calling again from upstairs—"Henry! Henery! You-all come up here, Henry!"—and she didn't sound awfully sober.

We went up. But first I looked at the book on the floor. It was the second volume of Tom Watson's "Story of France" and that was a funny one, too. Mrs. Boggs's favorite reading, I happened to know, was the funny papers and the financial page.

As soon as we showed at the door of her room, she started crying again. In a flossy nightgown and a jacket-thing with fur on it, she sat up in a four-poster bed full of pink pillows and cried like all forty. Henry sat on the edge of the bed and yelled at her.

"Hey, Maw, quit it!"

He shook her and she cried harder.

Henry stood up. He winked over his shoulder at us.

"All right," he said in a lull between sobs, "if you don't quit I'm goin' to town."

Mrs. Boggs stopped instantly.

Even then she couldn't tell us much more than Henry had. But you could see the cops were mightily impressed by all that bed and lace and her right arm bandaged to the elbow.

After dinner, she said, she was reclining on the lounge, reading, and Henry was in the next room dealing poker hands to himself. The servants were somewhere in the back washing the dishes. Maybe she fell asleep over her book—she wasn't sure—they'd had wine with dinner and wine always made her sleepy—but the first thing she knew there was a terrible noise and the window fell in on her and that's the last she knew till Henry woke her sloshing water on her. The glass had cut her arm something terrible and if it hadn't been for Henry, she would have bled to death.

With that she started sobbing again. Henry moved away from the bed and winked at us.

"Don't mind maw. She cries easy."

"Pour me a drink, honey," Mrs. Boggs whimpered, and Henry poured her one from a decanter at the side of the bed.

"Hadn't we better call a doctor, Miz Boggs?" one of the cops said.

"We already called one," Henry said quickly. "He'll be here directly."

Mrs. Boggs wiped her eyes on one of the dinky pillows. "Oh, no! Don't mind me," she sobbed. "Henry'll take care of me! You go after the dirty skunks that done this to me!"

As we went out, she yelled after us, "Assassims!—that's what they are—assassims!"

Well, the cops had the servants in, a nigger man and a nigger woman, scared gray and contradicting everybody and each other. "We'll run 'em both in on suspicion," the cops decided.

They hunted around the room till they found where the bullets went, both in the ceiling. They went outside, making me and Pete stay where we were for fear we'd mess up the ground. Henry was upstairs with mamma—we could hear him asking her for money; we heard him say, "Hell, Maw, you've always gotta grease the cops."

I said to Pete, "What do you think of this business?"

"Looks like somebody was after the old bat sure enough. And no wonder—after all the hell the Red Riders've raised."

"Yes," I said, "I guess that'll be what folks'll think. But she had other enemies. Maybe Mrs. Albert Sidney Johnston Green took a pot shot at her."

Pete laughed. Then a car drove up outside and George X. Jones hustled in, too excited to slink. He had the doctor with him.

"Where is she?"

"Upstairs," we told him, and he and the doctor went up.

Jones came down again in less than a minute. For a man who had just seen his Pythoness on a bed of pain, he wasn't exactly lugubrious.

"Well, boys, you've got a story!"—he rubbed his palms together like there were hot dice between them—"yes, sir, a whale of a story! The whole country's going to be shocked by this. They can talk all they please about a little rough stuff, but when assassins lurking in the dark attempt to shoot down innocent women in cold blood, it's time the American people woke up to the truth of what's going on. We're mighty lucky Mrs. Boggs didn't pay for her patriotism with her life tonight."

"So you think it was assassins, too?" I asked him.

"Certainly I do! Who else could it be? Mrs. Boggs, personally, didn't have an enemy in the world. She's the kindliest and most Christian of women—and you can quote me as saying that. Not an enemy in the world! But we all know there are powerful influences in this country who would rejoice—yes, rejoice, boys!—if the O-R-R was suddenly deprived of its splendid chieftainess." He held up one hand. "I'm making no charges!—please understand that. But it's as plain as the nose on your face. Directly or indirectly, the persons responsible for this monstrous attack are those responsible for the campaign of vilification and abuse against the O-R-R. If they can't win in the open, they'll strike in the dark!"

He was pleased as punch. Pete Barron took notes. I said, "Aren't you afraid for your own skin?"

"Ha!" he barked, "ha!" and he squeezed my arm. "We'll not worry about that, Dudley. Time enough to pick the pallbearers when you've got a corpse. In the meantime, how about a little drink? You fellows must be all in, hauled out on a big story in the middle of the night."

On the way to the kitchen, he was chuckling like a good fellow. "And where's the *Blade*? Behind the *Star* and the *Courier* as usual, I suppose!"

"Maybe nobody telephoned the *Blade*," I suggested.

The cops joined us in the kitchen. So did the doctor, one I never had seen or heard of before. He said Mrs. Boggs' wound was a painful laceration, but not serious. The cops said there were footprints outside the bay window and a scuffed spot behind a rhododendron bush where the assassin undoubtedly had stood. They'd traced the footprints to the road and found fresh tire marks in the edge of the lawn. We all had a drink and Pete Barron said he was going to telephone his story. I said I'd wait for him.

When I strolled into the dining-room, I was surprised to find Henry at the big table, dealing cards.

"Hello," I said, "I thought you were upstairs with your mamma."

"Passed out—the doc give her a shot."

"You're not drinking tonight?"

"Not with those punks!"

I thought to myself: what a little rat you are for all your swell clothes. But I sat down and said, "You mean the cops?"

He blubbed through his lips. "It goes for the cops, too."

"You surely don't mean our friend, Mr. Jones, do you?"

"That punk! He better lay off. If he starts anything with my sweet patootie—"

He went on shuffling the cards and I didn't say anything. Suddenly he brightened.

"How about a couple of cold hands for fifty cents, pal?"

"All right—you deal."

He dealt and won.

"Jones got a girl at the Palace now?" I said while he was shuffling.

"Cut," said Henry.

I cut and said, "His secretary's a pretty good looker."

"Kings over jacks," said Henry and took my fifty cents.

By the time Pete Barron returned, Henry had put seven dollars on my expense account and the paper was no wiser for it.

"Better luck next time, pal," was his good-by.

We rode to town not saying much. I dropped Pete at the *Star* office and fell asleep on the way home. The alarm clock said two-thirty when I turned in.

CHAPTER TEN

I N THE MORNING, WHEN I GOT TO THE OFFICE, THE clipping from the front page of the *Star* was in my typewriter:

ATTEMPT TO ASSASSINATE

RED RIDERS' QUEEN BEE

TWO SHOTS FIRED AT MRS. ROSEBUD BOGGS

Pete Barron's story ran for a column, including Jones' statement. It raised no doubts. It said the police were launching a "nation-wide manhunt" for the would-be assassins. It said arrests could be expected at any moment.

Deadwyler had written on the clipping, "See me."

"This thing's a phony," I told him.

"What makes you think so?"

"Well, there's a catch in it somewhere. A dame like Mrs. Boggs doesn't lie down after dinner to read a history of France and, if she does, she doesn't leave all the pages uncut. If she was lying on that lounge under that bay window, a person outside would have to be looking down at her instead of up at her to see her at all. And he would shoot down rather than up if he wanted to hit her. He wouldn't shoot bullet holes in the ceiling. Maybe flying glass from a busted window could cut her in one arm and nowhere else but I'd like to see the trick done. I'd like to see if there was any glass outside that window. I'd like to see that cut. Furthermore, I'd like to know who called George X. Jones and who called the papers before anybody called the police. Who called you, by the way?"

"Police. The desk sergeant has my home phone number."

"So have a lot of people. So has George X. Jones. Tell me this—why, when you 'phoned me, did you say Mrs. Boggs was 'assassinated'? Ordinarily you'd say she'd been 'killed' or 'murdered' or 'bumped off.' "

Deadwyler looked interested.

"Why, that's what the guy who 'phoned me said. He said, 'Mrs. Boggs has been assassinated.' So that's why I said the same thing to you. The word was in my head."

"Uh, huh. Well, if the police did 'phone you, the desk sergeant didn't get the word out of the dictionary. He got it from the *Star* and the *Star* got it from whoever phoned the *Star*. And George X. Jones had it when he reached the house, and Mrs. Boggs had it, only she couldn't pronounce it. Apparently somebody was awful anxious to make this an 'assassination' and not just a plain little two-bit shooting."

"What do you think?" said Deadwyler.

"I don't know what I think. I don't know whether George X. Jones hired somebody to shoot Mrs. Boggs or whether Henry shot at her or whether she shot the shots herself. I don't know if there was any shooting at all. But I'll bet a pretty, however it was, it was a grand-stand act."

"But why did they spring it?" asked Deadwyler. "Just to get Old Lady Boggs' picture in the papers?"

I thought a minute. "Yes and no. Have you heard the rumors that've been going around lately about the Red Riders? I don't mean the stuff that they'll be smashed by the next Congress or the stuff that they'll elect the next Congress—that's hogwash both ways. I mean about dissension inside the order. They say there's a fellow up North somewhere—Dread Scorpion of the West or something like that—who's raising hell with the Supreme Palace. They say he's trying to get Sloat and Jones deposed. They say he's got a lot of Riders from Indiana and Texas and Missouri and other states with him. They say he's putting it on moral grounds—Sloat being a boozer and so on—but I imagine it's a case of dog eat dog. He's smelled money and so have a lot of other Scorpions and Cobras and Tumblebugs. If they can convince the brothers that Sloat, Jones and Boggs are a bunch of grafters, they can grab control. But if Jones pacifies the rank and file, he's still riding pretty. He's already made a noble Roman of old Doc Sloat and now he's making a Nurse Cavell of Mrs. Boggs. Next thing you know we'll have him in the role of a Rollo boy."

We played the story down; that was orders from Colonel Cronkhite. But grand-stand act or not, it was still a two-bagger for the O-R-R. The big press associations wired the story just as it appeared in the *Star,* it was printed that way all over the country, and, sure enough, the Supreme Palace flooded the newspapers with bunk about the martyred Mrs. Boggs. Some of it was printed, too.

The O-R-R, which had been fading from the front pages since the *Sphere's* series ended and the Congressional investigation flopped, went back there big, this time in the role of victim and prosecutor instead of defendant. And though papers like the *Sphere* jeered the implication of dirty work by the O-R-R's foes, and though later stories cast doubts on the genuineness of the "assassination plot," the results must have been mighty pleasing to George X. Jones. I had no idea, then, that mere publicity was the least of the tricks he hoped to take.

The attempt on Mrs. Boggs' life—if you want to call it that— happened on the night of December 5. In two days she was fully recovered. By December 1 o the story had disappeared from the papers.

On December 15 the Supreme Palace of the Red Riders announced its first national Reptilon, to convene in Vesta January 1 with Red Riders present from forty-five states.

On December 26, the day after Christmas, the police of Gary, Indiana, arrested the Dread Scorpion of the Jungle of the Middle West.

The first dispatches from Gary were vague. They said only that R. E. Durkan, a labor boss and local politician, was held on suspicion in connection with the attempt to assassinate Mrs. Rosebud Boggs. Later dispatches amplified the description of Durkan. He had been arrested twice before, once for sabotage in a laundry strike and once by federal prohibition agents. Both times he beat the rap. In the underworld of Gary he was known as "Big Red," he was a power, reputed to be rich and to derive his money from bootlegging and various "protection" rackets. His eminence in the O-R-R was not mentioned—not for a week would the newspapers know he was even a member.

"I've been framed—send for my lawyer," was Durkan's not very original statement. He did not add to it, nor did he at once make bail, which was high because of the nature of the charge. When this was specified as conspiracy to murder, the Gary police declined details. The charge, they said, was brought by Vesta authorities, who would seek extradition. The Vesta authorities— meaning our own police—were equally clammy. They had the goods on the guy and you bet your life they weren't going to tip their mitts to the damn reporters!

So matters stood, as far as the newspapers and the public were concerned, when from Maine and California, from the great cities of the East, the crossroads of the plains, the backwoods and the hills—from every state in the union but three, Utah,

Minnesota and New Hampshire—concentrated on Vesta the King Cobras and Terrible Tarantulas, the Cockatrices, Hydras, Basilisks, Dragons, Sepsi, Dipsa and Ophi of the Veiled Legion of the Right Royal and Venerable Order of Red Riders, risen from their Jungles, Dens and Lairs at the command of their Supreme Serpent, on the brooding day of the weird week of the frightful month of the Red Rider Year LVII. Lord! Lord! How I would love to have heard Doctor Sloat dictate *that* proclamation!

They did not come as delegates do to most reunions and conventions, with bunting flying and bands playing and the brothers and comrades pouring from the special trains to march the streets and chant the songs and clap a kiss on every pretty girl they see. Nobody yelled, "Where's Elmer?" as the Red Riders rode to town. They came via the regular Pullmans and many in day-coaches, thin and beefy men, ruddy men and pasty, of no particular distinction from other travelers nodding in the smokers, of no special identity save a common wariness of eye and a tendency, when two by two, to mutter unintelligibly in corners. They resembled nobody except, perhaps, the Solons of the State legislature, who assemble once a year to spit tobacco juice and vote the way the power trust says. Holding their shiny or dingy bags, they dribbled through the station throngs and were lost in the city among the loiterers in hotel lobbies and the eaters in cafeterias.

Only in one place, the New Manton Hotel, was the imminence of the Reptilon apparent. Here was headquarters, testified by a big red banner above the façade, another over the entrance to the Palm Room and just inside a girl at a desk reading a magazine and regarding every intruder combatively. That was all. Occasionally an intruder, leaning close, spoke, and she spoke lowly back and he hurried away looking mysterious. But toward those who possessed no magic word she froze. A reporter?

Mr. Jones was preparing a statement for the press. The Reptilon? All information will have to come from Mr. Jones. Where was Mr. Jones? Really, she couldn't say.

We were disgusted—inclined to pitch the Reptilon into the hellbox along with yesterday's type. Who gave a hoot for old Doc Sloat's roughnecks? What possible news worth writing or printing could come from these shifty-faced, sinister fatheads who kept appearing and disappearing like so many sourgum detectives? That seedy fellow on the edge of the chair who gargled his Adam's apple every time the door revolved—was he here for the Reptilon? The sleek waddler leaving the girl now— was he a King Cobra or a drummer trying to date her? If you asked him, he would laugh. If you spoke to the seedy guy, he would say, "Brother, I'm a stranger here myself." ... Go out to the Supreme Palace? Mac Kelly went this morning. He got the front gate and a message, "Mr. Jones is sending a statement to your office."

Yet we were frantic, too. For we sensed a story here and we were not so shy of friends or tips that we did not have an inkling of what it was about. The word had come down the line! This was no ordinary convention to ring the welkin, elect officers and adjourn; grave doings were afoot and they were concerned, somehow, with the man under arrest in Gary. Before the Reptilon was over something was going to happen, something was going to be done that would effect not only him but the whole O-R-R. But what it was, and where and how it was coming to pass, we could not find out.

I know, now, that on the morning we fumed between the Manton Hotel and the Palace, getting nowhere fast, forces were gathering to make Vesta a grimmer battleground than a Democratic convention. I know, now, that in the halls around us and in the rooms over our heads men were meeting, whispering, swapping secrets and promises, swearing oaths that, however fantastic, meant action as practical as a called note.

In one room, twenty men from twenty different states heard a horse-doctor talk. He had been a doctor of medicine before he became a horse-doctor, haranguing the country on the merits of Indian Pete's Moccasin Oil, and he talked well. He spoke of demagoguery, oppression and intimidation, of espionage and blackmail, of licentiousness in high places, of misconduct, malfeasance and nonfeasance and the proud name of a noble Order dragged in the quagmires of lust and prostituted to the selfish schemes of degenerates. He described a Supreme Serpent misruling his empire with the mind of a sot, an Imperial Python using him as a puppet to wreck and pillage and ruin, a Pythoness abetting the Python with the wiles of a Delilah and the cruelties of a Borgia.

He did not speak of spoils. But the *New York Sphere* already had done that—one bottle magic water, $10; Supreme Treasury cut, $9.90—to him and to every hungering Red Rider who heard him.

"And what, men of the North, did these rats do when the Dread Scorpion of your domain, a brave and true Red Rider, discovered their treacheries and denounced them and threatened to destroy their domination?" said the horse-doctor. "They framed him! They cooked up a fake assassination, they sent out their spies to bribe witnesses and plant evidence, they tried to get him through the law because they were afraid to get him by the knife and the gun as you well know they have gotten other brave and true Red Riders—as they will get you, brothers, if you don't fix them first! But when they framed my friend, Red Durkan, they framed the wrong guy! He may not be here in the flesh, but his crowd is here and my crowd is here and we're with him to the last chip! The thing I ask you, men, is, 'Where does your crowd stand?' And remember—he who is not with us is against us!"

That is what the horse-doctor said, or something like it, to the King Cobras and Terrible Tarantulas and Dread Scorpions. He said it to many more that afternoon and night, and in other rooms of the Manton and in hotels all over the city the fine words of the horse-doctor were repeated and Red Riders swore over their bottles that the horse-doctor was right and they would no longer be the dupes of drunkards, thieves and whoremasters. A six-foot Texan, who had been a brakeman on the Santa Fe before he became Basilisk of Dallas Den No. 6, swore it to the Cockatrice of the Lair of Illinois, formerly a barber in Cicero. The barber patted a violin case, which did not hold a fiddle, and a Newark ex-policeman, King Cobra of the Jungle of the East, agreed with them both as he smoothed twin barrels of steel beneath an armpit.

That day, too, must have seen much pow-wow in the Supreme Palace, for some time before midnight George X. Jones arrived at the horse-doctor's rooms, bringing with him six bodyguards and a flag of truce. The bodyguards, it is said, were imported talent—killers of Frankie Yale's Brooklyn mob—and two at least were getting double pay, from the horse-doctor as well as Jones. They lined themselves along the wall while Jones spoke his piece.

"I want to trade," he said to the horse-doctor, and he offered him Sloat.

He offered him Sloat wrapped, tied and delivered—by impeachment or "leave of absence" or, if more convenient, in a pine box labeled "alcoholic poisoning"—and all he asked in exchange was a five years' contract as head of propagation for the O-R-R, with a cut, of course, of every joiner's fee.

"Why should I trade?" said the horse-doctor.

"Because," said Jones, "if you don't, the O-R-R is a dead cat. Who made it—Sloat? He's not smart enough, and you're not smart enough, and nobody in your gang's smart enough, to run the O-R-R without Jones. Try it and see."

"But why give me Sloat?" said the horse-doctor. "I've got him!" and he took from his pocket something the size of a postal card which he handed to George X. Jones.

"The negative," said the horse-doctor, "is locked in a vault a long, long way from here. But in twenty minutes I can lay my hand on a hundred more prints like that one. Go back and show it to Dr. Sloat. Ask him if he remembers Milwaukee. And tell him, if he has the gall to stand for renomination, we'll disgrace him before the convention!" I don't know what was on the post-card, but if the Doc was ever drunk in Milwaukee, I can imagine. "What do I want with Sloat?" said the horse-doctor. "You keep him—I don't like him!"

He leaned back, chuckling at George X. Jones, who must have looked pretty sick. I can imagine his red eyes flickering and the bodyguards shifting theirs from man to man, wondering which dog to bet on.

"No," said the horse-doctor, "you can't trade me Sloat—and you can't trade me Mrs. Boggs. There's going to be a new Supreme Serpent and a new Imperial Pythoness and I shouldn't wonder if there'll be a new Imperial Python—after tomorrow night. But speaking of Mrs. Boggs, maybe we can trade. Somebody tried to kill her, they say. Somebody put the finger on Big Red Durkan. Somebody's got to take the rap if he don't. Mr. Jones, maybe if you and me had a little talk in private, we could help the authorities find the guilty man."

The horse-doctor was smiling at the bodyguards when he said that, and not one of them smiled back. But they went out. When Jones joined them, he was smiling, too. He shook hands with the horse-doctor and walked ahead of them along the hall. Nobody was sure enough to shoot him in the back.

The morning of New Year's Eve broke gray and cold and before noon a drizzle was falling that changed to sleet as the day grew darker. Downtown Vesta was a sludge in which cars jammed and slithered and people glared as they banged against each other on the lee side of buildings. There's little New Year's Eve whoopee in a righteous town like ours and there would be less than ever tonight, I knew.

I wasn't bothering much about the Reptilon story. We'd all taken the handouts from the Supreme Palace—three typewritten pages of rhetoric that, boiled down, said the Red Riders would have a parade and elect officers "somewhere in Vesta" before midnight—and I'd gone over to the Manton to make a final checkup.

Nobody knew anything. I heard the parade had been called off. I heard the Reptilon would be held at the Supreme Palace and I heard it would be held on top of Crag Mountain. God help them if it is, I thought. I heard that Sloat would be succeeded as Supreme Serpent by a Texas dentist and I heard he would be re-elected for life and I said, "Oh, hell, who cares either way? You'd think this was as important as a meeting of the Vesta Women's Club!" and I went out into the mush to report back to the office.

Passing the Pelham Bank Building, I saw a cream-colored limousine in front and I edged under an awning and waited. Rain dripped, muddling the sleet underfoot, and I kept my collar up and my hat pulled down. Several other people stood under the awning. I looked twice at one of them and he was Henry, the Seattle Kid.

I started to speak, thought better of it and eased back a little. The Seattle Kid smoked, holding his cigarette with his hand before his face. His collar was up and his hat down like everybody else's.

When Jones passed us, coming out of the building, I didn't move. But when the Seattle Kid didn't either, I went out quick.

"Jones!" I yelled.

He whirled like a flash and I never saw a man so scared stiff. If his hat didn't rise on his hair, then call me a liar; his little eyes bugged and his right arm, holding his brief-case, went up as if he were going to hit me.

"What's the matter?" I said. "I just want some dope on the Reptilon. Are you really meeting on Crag Mountain?"

He swallowed twice before he could speak.

"What?—what? I'm in a hurry, Dudley. I can't stop to talk to you."

"Oh, all right, all right! But are you going to parade?"

"Can't discuss it!" he snapped, opened the door, pitched the brief-case into the back seat and jumped after it. The big limousine left me standing flat. I didn't even get a look at the driver. When I turned around, the Seattle Kid was gone.

But as I waited for traffic at the corner, a red sports model Buick splashed by and I remembered what somebody had said, that Mrs. Boggs had given her wandering boy a red sports model Buick for Christmas. This one was roaring like hell—from first into second—and picking up so fast I couldn't see who was in it.

"What's coming off here?" I thought. "Or are you getting the twitters as bad as a Terrible Tarantula?"

Back at the office, I had a sandwich and a dope-and-lime, telephoned some people about a party for that night and hung around for the home editions of the *Courier* and the *Blade.* I was telephoning again, to reserve a table for six at Jack's Rathskeller, when two things happened: the managing editor sent word he wanted to see me and the home edition of the *Blade* came up with a front-page scoop. Mrs. Boggs had sworn out a warrant for the arrest of Giorgio Vasco, who had skipped town before it could be served. The charge was attempt to murder.

I rewrote the story for the final edition and all the way home wondered what was behind it and the tip Mr. Roberts had given me.

"We know confidentially," he had said, "that George X. Jones drew a big sum of money from the bank today, considerably over half a million dollars. There may be trouble tonight—the police have been warned. You'd better stand by for a call and, if you're going out, leave word where you'll be."

All through dinner, while I was catnapping, while I dressed and after I reached the Rathskeller, I expected that call. It never came. But about ten-thirty, when the party was just beginning to warm up, I heard the fire gong. Fire headquarters is only two blocks from the Rathskeller; it has one of those old-fashioned alarms that sound so many strokes for each part of town and this was three strokes, for the north side. They were loud enough to penetrate a New Year's Eve party in the bad place.

I called our waiter, who was a good nigger, and told him to find out where the fire was. He came back after a few minutes, grinning with every tooth.

"Out River Road at de ole Smith place," he said, "an' dey say it's a big 'un!"

I'd remembered my overcoat but forgotten my hat when I hit the street. The sleet had stopped, but the sky was like black mud except away to the north where you could imagine an orange glare.

CHAPTER ELEVEN

THESE THINGS I DID NOT SEE ....

The parade of the Red Riders. Despite rain and sleet, they marched.

They formed in the old baseball grounds in De Soto Park where, by late afternoon, an increasing number of men, bearing parcels like so many home-going husbands, streamed through the rickety gates. Under the stands, next day, small boys would discover drained flasks, cigar butts, copies of the *Cyclops,* a torn coat and a trampled hat—two masks; one red, one white—as witnesses that here the magic alchemy took place. Out there, from home plate to center field, the Veiled Legion stood. The empty bleachers looked down on a thousand robed, cowled figures; through gaps in the sagging fence the torches flared. From that grandstand box, long after dark, leaped the fiery serpent and boomed the battle cry.

The folk of Happy Hollow saw them coming first. This is a Negro section outside the park—a scrabble of shanties and chillun and fleabitten dogs, living on without even the hope of a foul ball skied among them any more. You can imagine eyeballs rolling at the spectacle; or, more likely, since the Hollow is an aware community, not a light showing nor a hound's nose as the red hoods flowed by.

Then the white families up the hill. They were at supper when the bugle rang. "The Riders!" From the porches of bungalows and the windows of jerry-built apartments they stared, shivering a little in the damp cold. Mamma and the kids; papa, who talked more about the office than politics and had never joined "a lodge," but who was an authority on affairs just the same. There would be argument after the meat balls and the rice pudding in the great American home … "Well, maybe it's a good thing; those niggers down there so close to us!"

The parade, moving up De Soto Heights, passed more apartments, more bungalows and finer homes. Judge Prescott Winship, who lost an arm at Resaca but lived to plow his own field after the surrender, sighed and turned a little sadly from his window to his speech on law enforcement for the Bar Association banquet. His neighbor, Keith Pelham, likewise sighed, reminded of the day's withdrawals from the Pelham National Bank.

Harvey P. Douglas, no cavalier of the old South yet another "first citizen," saw the parade and generously cursed the police, the mayor and the damn politicians. The chief of police saw the parade and telephoned his lieutenants, "Tell the boys to go easy, but we won't stand for no monkey business." The mayor saw the parade and counted votes for the next election. Several aldermen saw the parade after dropping out of line. In the Terrace Hotel, some Easterners watched through the windows of the sun garden and one of them, as she looked on the Red Riders from every state save three, said, "Isn't the South too queer!"

Here, at the corner of De Soto Street and Manton Avenue, the parade swung north. Three blocks farther, waiting automobiles picked up the marchers.

Kerosene torches, burning like sacred fires before the temple, lit the desolate slopes around the Supreme Palace. Through the unchained gates they poured. Past the masked seneschals who lifted, then dropped, each mask. Across the vaulted lobby where the great red cobra squirmed among the tiles. Up the grand staircase. The banners billowed, the shields flashed, the crystal chandelier shook its prisms. Said a Hydra from Delaware to the Dragon of Toledo Den No. 2, "Some dump!"

On the top floor, where the Grand Reptilium ranged the length and breadth of the building, four "Terrors" in the four corners of the hall held high their fiery serpents. A fifth "Terror," with a fifth torch, guarded the altar with its huge American flag. In this murk, where a man could not read the stencils on the chairbacks ("Return to J. P. Gibson's Mortuary Parlors"), let alone recognize his brother, the host seemed void of leadership. Yet, as it spread and congealed, a tremor ran through it and there were apparent a pattern and a guide.

So the hoods settled, swayed—upraised toward the platform and the flag. And now the sentinel ceased to pace before the altar, silence fell and from the flag's folds stepped one all in crimson. As his hand went up, he cried out, "Cum clab ad Clastra!"

You can imagine, knowing what was to follow, the bowels of the Palace some moments before this and the Imperial Python, George X. Jones, clad in the regalia of the Supreme Serpent, bending over Dr. Sloat.

You can imagine the old man far gone in liquor ... giggling foolishly, croaking hymns, mouthing his words ... "Man's inhumanity to man makes countless millions—"

"Sign it!" says Jones, and shakes him cruelly.

You can imagine the extended paper as Sloat's abdication; his power of attorney, his conveyance of deed, his last will and testament; in any event, his relinquishment of all rights in the Ancient and Venerable Order of Red Riders.

"Sign it, you fool!"

The old man will not sign.

"Christ save me from drunkards!" says Jones and straightens up, the crimson robes cumbersome about him, the fox head poking from the hood like a sweating skull.

"Give him another shot," he says.

The hand may be a man's or a woman's that forces the glass against the lips until they belch and drool. But if it is a man's, it is not Ganymede's, for Buck chases other fox tonight. And if it is a woman's, it is not Mrs. Boggs'. She waits uncertainly at Roselands.

"Doggoneit," says Jones, too tired to blaspheme.

A bell rings somewhere in the crypt.

"Doggoneit," he repeats.

You can imagine, then, the Imperial Python adjusting his hood, clutching a brief-case beneath the robe and faring forth to put his luck to the touch.

The struggle for control of the Red Riders at this hour seems, in the light of post-revelations, to have reached something of a deadlock.

The horse-doctor had the votes and, by his simple use of blackmail, the whiphand. But the founding triumvirate had possession, which was nine points of the law, and the all-important tenth point, the charter. If the horse-doctor moved too ruthlessly, he might gain a temporary victory but lose all in the courts. And if the triumvirate resisted too arrogantly, they might sacrifice a million members and ten times as many dollars. Either way, the Order risked ruin. The golden goose stretched its neck on the block; it was a time for counsel and compromise.

Earlier in the day, therefore, Jones had appeared to Dr. Sloat and Mrs. Boggs with a proposition. He said it was the horse-doctor's—a statement that is open to doubt, since he urged them to accept it. But if it was not altogether the horse-doctor's, we can believe it was in part—trimmed and colored to suit Jones' natural bent for trickery and whatever private deal to his own advantage the horse-doctor had proffered him.

Sell out to the rebels and they would all be rich for life! That was the proposition. Conditions were demanded—they must quit the Red Riders finally and forever, they must start no other fraternal order and—oh, yes! a minor item—they must provide a scapegoat. Mr. Red Durkan disliked jail, a victim must be found to pay for the sins of which Mr. Durkan was accused, and Mr. Jones had a suggestion. After all—he smirked—nobody liked foreigners.

We may be sure that the minor item was quickly approved, even by Mrs. Boggs. Before noon, she had signed the complaint against Vasco.

But the major motion was something else. Suspicion and contention charged the conference and argument was long and bitter. Before adjournment—so wily and acrimonious were the confreres—each must have in his own witness, Mrs. Boggs her son, Jones his secretary and Dr. Sloat his friend, Gabe Trippy, who would sooner have turned the dispute into a hymn-sing, but recognized that his bread and whiskey hung in the balance. The three seconds, listening a lot and saying little, in the end swung the tide.

Miss Gobbett, having remarked that her boss was generally right and cash money in hand was better than fighting a buzz-saw in the bush, turned suddenly and asked Henry if he didn't agree. To everyone's surprise, the Seattle Kid, who had come in glaring at Jones, said he did.

"Listen, Maw," he urged Mrs. Boggs, adamant hitherto to all persuasions, "remember what them Moodys done to you when you was rich before—don't mess with lawyers! We don't want no court-suits, the lawyers'll git it all. Grab what you can and breeze—that's what smart hoboes do."

"The lad is right," Reverend Trippy broke in. " 'Beware of men, for they will deliver you up to the councils and they will scourge you in their synagogues.' " This was for Sloat, who had evidently seen the postal-card. "Let us be wise as serpents and harmless as doves. The Bible says, 'When they persecute you in this city, flee ye into another.' Better take the advice of the Good Book, Sim. Sell out!"

The Doctor roared. Sell out to the heathen? To those ingrates and traitors? To those durn skunks?—Smash the dream of a lifetime? Forget the ambition of his youth and the fulfillment of his old age?—Why, when he was a child, walking across the battlefield of Gettysburg—and he gave them his stuff.

Moreover, he concluded, the price was ridiculous. Chickenfeed! Why, he had poured the Sloat millions into the O-R-R and he was not going to quit for a measly three hundred thousand. With that he smiled benignantly on Jones, the genii to the "Simeon D. Sloat Foundation," whose expression you can imagine.

The conference, thereupon getting down to turkey, at length broke up in seeming harmony. Jones was to return to the horse-doctor with a counter-proposition; they would buy off the horse-doctor or demand a higher ante. If this move failed—well, they could always stand pat and fight.

Everyone shook hands on it, someone doubtless quoted, "If we don't hang together, we shall all hang separately," and Mrs. Boggs was so distracted she put her name to several checks Jones suggested might be necessary for the negotiations. You can picture them, then, scattering in the common resolve to diddle each other, Jones toward the city, Mrs. Boggs toward Roselands, the Doctor mournfully to liquid consolation in his snuggery, the seconds considerably churned up after exposure to the dasher of nearly a million dollars.

That—as nearly as I can figure—is about what happened. But before Jones met the horse-doctor again, we know he was followed to the bank. We know at least one person saw him leave it. There may have been more.

You can believe, when he locked Sloat in the crypt and climbed the secret stairway which, it was afterward discovered, led to a trapdoor in the stage of the grand reptilium, that he was still playing fair with both sides and had determined to go through with the deal minus Sloat's signature, prevailing over the Supreme Serpent when he was sober.

You can believe that he had decided to abandon Sloat—and maybe Mrs. Boggs to boot—cheat them by forgery or force and throw in his lot with the horse-doctor.

Or you can believe that he was the lone wolf, about to seize the Supreme Serpency, fight rebels and masters both, and set up a new hierarchy.

Personally, I do not believe any of these things. As Jones rose behind the flag through which the torches and the shadows flickered, I believe he was a man in a muddle. He did not know which way the cat would jump. But, caught between the grindstones of insurrection and treason, he had prepared to jump, too. That was his blunder. Like Irene Adler in "A Scandal in Bohemia," rushing to save her treasure at the first cry of calamity, he had betrayed himself to his Sherlock Holmes. A score of men in the hall must have known he had drawn half a million dollars that day. Probably they suspected he had it on him. The horse-doctor must have known and he must have burned with distrust and greed.

I feel just a little bit sorry for Jones. When he faced them—Frankenstein versus the monster—he surely knew himself a fool to be there. He thought, now, of something more valuable to him than money—his neck. But we shall never know precisely what he thought, for, as "Cum clab ad Clastra!" bellowed from his lungs, somebody shot him.

I say somebody shot him and yet not all the detectives in Chatauga County, nor I, can swear to that. "They" say Jones did not swerve nor stagger as the gun blazed. "They" say there was no blood on the stage or on the secret stairway, though fire may have burned the drops away, and there was no blood within or without the automobile in which he fled. "They" say he was not shot, but simply shot at.

Certainly, a shot was fired and possibly more than one. Whether they came from the front of the hall or the back, whether from one gun or many, no man testifies. Nor why a shot was fired. There is a story that the horse-doctor, afraid he would lose, deliberately instigated a riot. There is a story that gunmen hired to kill Sloat not unnaturally mistook Jones for their man. There is a story that a giant leaped from the masked rows, threw off his hood, exposing his red head, and cried, "There's the son-of-a-bitch framed me!" before he fired.

Take your pick. It is a fact that Big Red Durkan, freed on bail, was not seen in Gary for twenty-four hours before or after the Vesta Reptilon.

A shot was fired …. Immediately, confusion in the hall was indescribable. Men scrambled for the stage. Men scrambled for safety. Men fought. They gouged at each other's masks and struggled to keep on their own. Grappling, they rolled among the chairs, kicking the faces beneath them. A fiery serpent tipped from a "Terror's" arms and lit among the mob, burning men who screamed. Another, bubbling oil, banged into the flag. It burst ablaze and whoever beat at it seemed to blaze; too, and, running, to spread the flames. "They" also say the fire was incendiary— madmen hurling torches at texture in a frenzy of destruction. In the moment before the fire got its hold the hall was hugger-mugger. Through it a flying wedge of Riders charged. When they reached the stage, they found neither Jones nor his body.

❧   ❧   ❧

Riding north, we could see the glow ten miles away. The roof of the Supreme Palace looked like a beautiful volcano as we neared it and the closer we came the higher she seemed to spout. We passed a hook-and-ladder and two hose-trucks and I don't know how many other cars, all heading hell-for-breakfast to the big show.

When we got there, cars were parked for a hundred yards ahead and the fence around the Palace looked like the sidelines at a football game. It was cold as hell—you could have skated on the road, trees and bushes were shags of crystal—but the spectators perspired and the heat melted icicles under our hands.

I saw the Fire Chief's red wagon near the gates. He stood in the drive, just staring at the roaring pyre where old Jasper Smith had expected the Smiths of the world to congregate.

"Can't do anything till the water comes," he said. "If there's anybody in that nuthouse he's a gone coot."

I thought about Dr. Sloat tippling and singing in the crypt and I wondered if, when the fire broke out, he'd had the sense and legs to run.

But my job was to do more than stand and stare. What started the fire? Who was in the Palace when it started? Where were they now? Where was George X. Jones, that arch-giver-out of statements? I looked around. The faces stark in the glare were not all known to me, yet they were familiar faces. I was sure they were, in the main, home-town folk. Where, as their capital burned, were the Red Riders of America?

A siren, moaning from the south in the wake of the fire engines, brought the answer. A dozen motorcycle policemen bucked and backfired and yelled at the crowd filling the road. They were not stopping, they were going through. I ran to one momentarily blocked and risked a broken head until he gave me the dope with his curses. Then I sprinted back to George Lester in his car.

"Get going!" I told him. "All hell's busted loose!"

George is a swell fellow. In 1915, when the *Lusitania* sank, he'd gone to Canada to enlist without telling his family good-by, and he'd run bareheaded out of the Rathskeller with me at the first alarm. While he drove, I talked.

"The whole shooting match was out here tonight holding their Reptilon. Something happened to break it up and they all lit out in their automobiles about time the fire began. They're after somebody—maybe the guy that set the fire. Anyhow, everybody on River Road has telephoned the police that big trouble was heading toward Mrs. Boggs' place!"

CHAPTER TWELVE

TWO CORPSES WELCOMED US AT ROSELANDS.

George X. Jones was dead in the driveway, a bullet hole through his forehead and another over his heart.

Mrs. Rosebud Boggs lay face down in her living-room. She had been shot three times in the back.

Vasco, the police said, was their murderer.

They had arrested two material witnesses. Wanda Gobbett sat with a cop in the dining-room and clawed at her hair while she cried. When she gibbered words, they didn't make sense. Henry was in the kitchen with another cop. He was white as fat-meat and looked scared, but his hand didn't shake as he lit his cigarettes.

"What's happened?" I asked both cops.

"See the lieutenant," they both said.

There seemed to be cops all over the house, none of them the lieutenant. There were other men, too, scores of them, gawking at the bodies, huddled in corners, on the stairs and out on the lawn. I saw several red robes when I first got there, but in fifteen minutes they'd vanished like bubbles off soda water.

When I couldn't find the lieutenant, I took another look at the dead.

Jones died flat on his back, his legs and arms flung out as if he'd been staked by Indians. So many cars had come into the drive and onto the lawn that their lamps flooded him like spotlights in a theater. There wasn't much blood—a big clot under his head that might have come more from a crack when he fell than from the bullet wound, another ooze showing on his left side where somebody had pulled back his overcoat, coat and shirt. The cops wouldn't let me look close. I wanted to see his hands. As I peered down at the empty palms, I kept thinking of him as I last saw him alive, humping out of the bank and suddenly popeyed with fear when I called his name.

"That's his car right there," a cop said. "He musta got it just after he hopped out."

I recognized the cream-colored limousine. It stood about six feet away, both doors open.

"Was anybody with him?"

The cop didn't know.

Back in the house, I didn't look long at Mrs. Boggs. Maybe it was the warm room, or because she was fat, that she'd bled so. I was glad when a cop put a sheet over her. Plenty of men had seen Rosebud Boggs disheveled in life, but somehow it seemed shameful that they should goggle at her in helpless death.

Another cop came out and asked me if I was the reporter, and when I said yes, he said the lieutenant wanted to see me.

The lieutenant was upstairs in a sort of library-office reached through Mrs. Boggs' bedroom, which gave me a queer feeling to walk through. Those lace pillows were piled so frivolously on the bed, and a French doll, with very black eyelashes and red lips, was cocked in the middle of them. The doll seemed awfully alive.

There was another man with the lieutenant—a heavy, pale man with heavy brows and pale eyes that never flicked as long as you met his gaze. In the face he looked like Napoleon, noble and evil, and in the body like Jess Willard two years after Dempsey knocked him out. This was the horse-doctor. But I didn't know it then.

I knew the lieutenant.

"Hi, Dudley," he said. "Sit down."

I took the third chair and said, "What's the dope?"

"You got it all, I reckon. No mystery for the papers this time. You knew they'd swore out a warrant for Vasco? There's your motive. He'd bungled the business before and when he heard they had the goods on him he made up his mind not to miss again. Get 'em both and get 'em good. He laid for Jones in the bushes and give it to him when he got outa the car. Then he runs in the house and gives it to Miz Boggs. The girl saw him."

"Miss Gobbett?"

"Miss Gobbett. Wanda Gobbett or some such name. She was his seckatary. Likewise, judgin' by the way she's been carryin' on, his sweetie. She was in the car when Jones was shot."

"How'd she happen to be in the car?"

The lieutenant glanced at the big man.

"Well, it's like I said—she was his seckatary. You knew they were havin' this big turnout at the Palace tonight. You know all about that. You worked for 'em once, didn't you?"

I felt pale eyes on me, curious and unwinking. "Not recently."

"Well, anyhow, Jones was at the Palace and it seems she was there, too, waitin' for him to get through. We haven't got it all out of her yet. When he come downstairs, they drove straight out here. That's the way we figure it, for it wasn't half an hour from the time they left the Palace till this gentleman and some of his friends run onto the Gobbett woman, standin' in the drive tearin' her hair and screamin', and Jones dead at her feet."

That was my cue to turn to the gentleman. He took an unlighted cigar from his mouth and said as cool as iced butter, "We were following them to pay our respects to the Supreme Pythoness. If we had known the road a little better, we might have arrived in time to avert the tragedy."

I said, "Did you leave before or after the fire started?"

He inspected me as if he were sizing up my capacity for being fooled or trusted, as if he were about to say, "What fire?" or to confide a terrific truth. He said, wetting the cigar, "Before."

"Then you don't know how it started?"

"No. We will make an investigation, of course. We will have a statement for the press."

"You mean the Red Riders? Are you a Red Rider? Who are you, anyway?"

"Now look here, Dudley," began the lieutenant.

The big man interrupted smoothly—"It's a fair question and I'll make a fair answer. I am a Red Rider, Mr. Dudley. So are many other gentlemen you see downstairs. But my individual identity—and theirs—is a matter of importance to nobody except the police. We have been perfectly frank with the police. We shall continue to co-operate with them in every way. Naturally, the Red Riders of the country will be the first to be outraged by this crime and to move heaven and earth to see justice done."

I took the liberty of doubting that statement, but I didn't say so.

The lieutenant began to bluster a little. "I'm giving you the facts, Dudley. It's none of your business where I get 'em. This gentleman, here, has been mighty helpful. If I have anything the papers ought to know, you'll get it, see?"

"All right—all right. I'm not riding you, am I? The *Courier's* not riding the police. I suppose it's all right if I talk to Gobbett and that kid of Mrs. Boggs? Where was he tonight?"

"In back. He heard the shots, but he didn't see nobody. When he got to his ma, it was too late. It was him called headquarters." He drummed with his fingers, not looking at the big man. "I reckon it's all right if you interview 'em."

I got up. "Thanks. Did Vasco make a clean getaway?"

"Through the woods, we think. Leastways, nobody saw or heard a car. But they'll get him. The sheriff's already swore out a posse."

"The sheriff? Was he here, too?"

The lieutenant looked embarrassed. I happened to know Sheriff Maples was as red a Rider as there was in the county.

"He got here," said the lieutenant, "almost as quick as me and my men did."

"Gosh," I said, "the sheriff and I must have driven up practically together!"

I couldn't resist that crack, but I was thinking privately: if Maples was here, that means the whole posse's composed of Red Riders. God help Vasco!

I went downstairs and tried to get Deadwyler on the telephone and finally got Mr. Roberts. He was at a New Year's Eve party and I could hear the bells and whistles and people yelling and somebody trying to sing "Auld Lang Syne." It was just midnight; at the Rathskeller our bunch would be going strong. But I didn't care; Mr. Roberts said to 'phone him at the office before five and we'd have an extra out by seven.

Henry was matching dimes with the cop when I walked in the kitchen. He had a little pile of dimes in front of him and the cop had twenty cents.

"Hi, pal," he said. "Feelin' lucky?"

I asked him about the murders.

"I'll tell you, pal, when I've told my lawyer."

"Come on!—you can tell me what you told the lieutenant."

"Okay, pal—I'll tell you what I told the lieutenant—nothin'!"

"He said you said you were in the back."

"Did he?"

"He said you didn't see Vasco."

"Cops do a lot of yappin', don't they? Beggin' *your* pardon, chief."

The cop went on chewing tobacco.

"He said you were the first to reach your mother after she was shot."

"Lay off my mother, pal," said Henry.

"Did she say anything before she died?"

Henry plumped two words, addressed to "Jack."

"Print that in your paper!" he said. He was a right hard little guy.

I asked him, "How many shots did you hear?"

"You match me," he said to the cop and spun a coin and slapped it. I waited till he won the cop's last dime.

"What do you suppose," I said, "they think you had to do with the murders? Come to remember, you never did like Jones."

He whirled around—"Easy, there!" the cop said—and then he began to cuss. He cussed me and he cussed the police and he cussed Vasco. He cussed Jones. He cussed the papers. He cussed the Red Riders. He cussed everybody but his mother. But mostly he cussed me.

"Thanks," I said. "Can I quote you?"

He told me what I could do as I went out. Yes, sir, he was a right hard little guy.

Wanda Gobbett, slumped over the big table in the dining-room, began to cry as soon as she saw me.

"Oh, Frankie! Oh, Frankie! Don't put me in the paper, Frankie! Please don't!"

Nobody's called me Frankie since I went to grammar school. I sat down feeling embarrassed and sorry for her, with a picture in my head of a big yard at recess and a lot of little boys and girls playing prisoner's base. But I couldn't help thinking how bossy and smartaleck she was then, switching her skirts, and how ugly she was now. She cried like a baby sometimes cries, without a tear and its face scrunched up. All the time she kept yanking at her hair.

"Look here," I said, "I can't help putting you in the paper. This is a big story and you're an eyewitness. If I don't, somebody else will. Better tell me all you know and I'll give you a break."

"But I don't know anything! Oh, my God, what'll my folks think!"

I wanted to say: You didn't give a damn what your folks thought when you played around with that preacher five years ago; you didn't give a damn when you rode out here tonight with Jones. I said, "Well, they're bound to find out. This thing will be in every paper in the country. Tell you what—I'll send somebody out there to break it to them gently. You don't want them hearing it from the neighbors first."

So she gave me their names and told me where they lived and the next day the *Courier* mopped up on Wanda's pictures.

But I did give her a break.

"Miss Gobbett, held as a material witness," said our story, "was the innocent victim of circumstances. A church member and former leader of the Epworth League, she had been Jones' secretary for several months. Last night she worked late and waited for him in his car outside the Palace. When he appeared, nervous and excited and apparently even then fearing foul play, he ordered her to drive to Roselands. On the way there, he told her something was wrong but refused to confide what it was. They stopped in the driveway and Jones leaped out. Miss Gobbett saw a shadowy figure rise from the underbrush, she heard a double report and a moment later, after Jones fell, three more shots. She was prostrated by her experience."

Mac Kelly, who took the facts over the phone, gave Wanda more than I asked for.

It wasn't exactly like that.

As long as the cop was listening, she wept and sniveled, but when he got up to get a drink of water, she leaned close and dug her fingers in my knee and her eyes were dry as chips.

"Listen, Frankie, George was scared! He was scared this afternoon before the parade. He was scared to death!"

"Of Vasco?"

She shook her head.

"Sh-h-h-h-h, they mustn't hear us. He was scared of—them. They'd threatened him. He went down to the grand crypt and Dr. Sloat was drunk and he said, 'God help us all if I can't get him sober!' "

"Well, if he didn't, the Doc's a cinder by now."

She paid no attention.

"Listen, Frankie—while I was waiting outside the Palace, something happened. I heard shots and then George came running out so scared he couldn't talk. They'd tried to kill him, Frankie! They were after him!"

"But dammit, you said Vasco did it!"

She stared, big-eyed.

"Didn't you say that? Didn't you tell the cops that? Didn't you say you saw Vasco jump out of the bushes and shoot Jones and then, after he ran in the house, you heard three more shots? Didn't you?"

She began to moan and cry—"Oh, I don't know! It all happened so sudden! Yes—there was somebody—I think it was Vasco—it was, it was Vasco! But I don't know, I don't know!"—and she went to tearing her hair again.

The cop was back.

"How about the fire?" I asked her. "Had the fire started before you-all beat it?"

"I don't know! I don't know anything about any fire."

"Well, there was a helluva big one. When I saw it, it looked like everything in the Supreme Palace was gone."

She snuffled something about her galoshes and the cold cream in her desk and I decided it might be a good idea to catch some fresh air.

Only a few cops were around besides those on guard, and no Red Riders. After the gang that had been all over the place when we got there, Roselands looked as empty and bright as a morgue.

"Where's all the folks?" I said to the cop who dozed in the front room with his feet slung across the sheet from one chair to another. He just jerked his head.

Outside, the dark was lightening, but the cold had a cemetery feel and the shrubbery, heavy with sleet, creaked like ghosts. I found George Lester huddled over the wheel of his car, sound asleep, and I woke him and told him all I knew. It was good to talk to a human being you could believe and who would believe you.

"Shucks," I said, "I don't know who to believe! The cops say Vasco did it. Wanda Gobbett says maybe he did and maybe he didn't. She says maybe the Red Riders did it. She seems to want to lay it on everybody. Where the hell are the Red Riders, anyhow?"

"Don't you know?" said George Lester. "They've gone after the money."

"What money?"

"The half a million dollars Jones had and Vasco stole."

I let my cigarette burn down to my fingers.

"Damn! ... So that story's out. I thought I was the only one knew it. I've been scared to ask anybody if Jones had a brief-case with him."

"You and who else knew it? Only about five hundred tough babies scouring the swamps between here and the river. What do you think I've been doing while you were fiddling around in there with a lot of dumb cops and dead bodies? I've been playing King Cobra. It's easy in the dark. All you do is slide up to another Cobra and hiss, 'Brother, do you want a drink?' That, my boy, is the password of the Red Riders. Unlocks all doors. So, while you chat with your sweetie in a nice, warm room, I freeze my feet and trade off my good liquor and get your story for you! And for what? You hold out on me a half a million dollars!"

"Never mind about my sweetie. What's the story?"

"What story? Vasco shot Jones, then Jones shot Ma Boggs and then Ma Boggs shot all the Red Riders. Who the hell cares who shot who? Over in those canebrakes there's a half a million dollars running loose and you sit here worrying about a story! Let's go, boy!"

"Hold your horses—how do you know any such thing?"

"They told me, the King Cobras told me! At least, they talked about it—hell, they couldn't talk about anything else!—and what I didn't hear, I guessed. They knew Jones took it out of the bank. They knew he had it—they saw it on him when he blew—and they hotfooted after him, the whole caboodle. That's what they were all doing here when we drove up, hunting for the dough. Maybe Vasco shot Jones and Ma Boggs—maybe the Red Riders shot 'em—I dunno—but somebody lit out with a half a million dollars and I move we go help 'em find it!"

I looked through the misty wind-shield at the hedges white in the dawn and the thick woods beyond them, and I thought of the miles of woods and swamp and canebrakes between us and the river—country where hounds tree many a 'possum that's never baked—and I said out loud, "They'll never find it tonight!"

They didn't, either. They found Vasco. They found him dead in a gully near Planter's Bridge, which he might have reached in two hours' hard running from Roselands. They found him with his own knife in his back and his head bashed in and one eye so mutilated it might as well have been none—a circumstance which could have pointed, but never did, to a certain member of the "posse." Officially, the posse killed him—and why not, since he was fleeing from foul murder? But they found no half million dollars. Not on Vasco or anywhere else. Not that night or ever.

George Lester and I didn't join the chase. We went back in the house, where we located a drink, and I telephoned my story, and after that we had several more drinks and the *Courier* had scooped the town by the time George turned his car toward home.

The Supreme Palace still smoked when we came in sight.

We stopped the car at the top of the hill and got out and talked to the firemen. They'd swung her under control, they said, before she completely gutted the place, but things were still too hot to work close and what the damage was or how many dead they couldn't say. If a cat could live in that oven, they claimed, it not only had nine lives but a fire-proof hole.

"Maybe there was one, at that," I said, "in the grand crypt. It was sound-proof."

There was a big shout about then, and people went running toward the Palace, and we ran and the firemen ran. I thought walls were falling, but they weren't. That sound was axes. The crowd was big and the police pushed them back and we couldn't see much, but pretty soon there were more shouts, "They've got him!"—"He's alive!"—"Well, by God, did you ever!"—and in another minute, when there came a little hush, I heard a voice.

It sang, or tried to sing, "Amazing grace, how sweet the sound—"

We scooped the town on Dr. Sloat's rescue, too.

CHAPTER THIRTEEN

I N THAT SLACK HOUR IN THE NEWSPAPER OFFICES of America when hooks are bare of copy and no chore remains save to listen to the old-timers until the presses roll, they may talk in other cities of renowned criminals and crimes, of their Hauptmanns and Leopolds and Hickmans and Capones, but in Vesta, though our front pages have never lacked either violence or glamour, one sturdy enigma persists as the bragging begins.

What is the true story of the Roselands tragedies, back there in the hazy days of Harding, before the country knew Coolidge prosperity or Hoover depression or Roosevelt revolution, when O-R-R, blazing through the headlines, meant as much in its fashion as WPA does today? Who killed George X. Jones and Rosebud Boggs?

The old reporter who covered the inquest and the famous double funeral where Red Riders marched six abreast behind the crimson caskets and stood, hoodless and defiant, while their Imperial Python and Pythoness were buried under cascades of roses, will tell you that the coroner was a fool. Only a fool or a crook would have accepted that verdict from his jury: "Murdered by Giorgio Vasco, deceased."

Why—says he—Vasco was no more guilty than Sloat, unconscious in the crypt! The sheriff's testimony? The sheriff lied when he said the posse tracked down Vasco, killed him "resisting arrest." Vasco was murdered in town and his body dumped at the bridge. He was never near Rose-lands that night. And his murderers—those "parties unknown"—were likewise the murderers of Jones and Mrs. Boggs. They would have murdered Sloat, too, but for the fire.

"Yes, sir," says the old reporter. "The Red Riders killed all three as sure as God made little apples!"

Another old-timer hoots. (This is one who saw the horse-doctor weep as the last rose shattered on the sod.) Vasco killed and was killed exactly as the evidence read. Didn't the Gobbett girl identify him? Didn't the Boggs kid partially identify him? Didn't members of the posse swear that Vasco, before he died, confessed and called for a priest?

"Rats!" snorts the old reporter, "the Red Riders spread that, trying to make it look like a Catholic plot!"

So it goes in the city room after fifteen years.

When they ask me, I must answer honestly, I don't know. Maybe it was the Red Riders, maybe it was Vasco. But when I think of that night—those two sprawled corpses, dry-eyed Wanda Gobbett, Henry in the kitchen matching dimes and cussing everybody but his mamma—I wonder. If Vasco was there, did he throw away his gun in the swamps? It was never found. Did bullets of the same bore kill Jones and Mrs. Boggs? The police said so. When Jones was shot, was he necessarily shot from the bushes? Might he not have been shot from the house—or the car? If Mrs. Boggs, in the house, heard the shots and ran toward the door, why was she shot IN THE BACK? Henry was her sole heir. Was he the sort that believes a boy's best friend is his mother? And do women ever really TEAR THEIR HAIR except in movies?

If this were a detective story, I could fit all those pieces neatly together and reveal as the murderer someone you never suspected, for choice Mrs. Albert Sidney Johnston Green. Unfortunately, I can only leave the facts in your lap.

I can't even tell you what became of the half million dollars. Treasure hunters still root in the canebrakes along the Chatauga, and perhaps it is there, rotting in Jones' brief-case under the mud and the moccasins. But I would give a lot to know whatever became of Wanda and Henry. If I ever read in a New York paper that Mr. and Mrs. H. Boggs were arrested for brawling in the Ritz, or that Henry tossed her off his yacht at Cannes, I'll feel a lot surer about the money and the murders.

Of the rulers and favorites of a fallen dynasty, only one, Dr. Sloat, remains in Vesta. He was a popular hero for a while after the fire. If he told his story once, he told it a thousand times, improving on it with each repetition until, instead of a drunk in a stupor saved by grace of granite foundations, he was Shadrach in the fiery furnace, praying to his God. Eventually he had the crypt full of angels and Moses in person striking water from the walls.

They expelled Dr. Sloat from the Red Riders. His impeachment was accomplished without commotion though I dare say not without cash. For a time he was a brave figure in the town's boozeries, where any patient listener could drink his health without cost. But inevitably, with no queen of her sex to boss his manners and no Jones to replenish his jug, he sank into the sad old ways. I saw him the other day, his planter's hat a-spraddle his ears, a cane across his arm and most of him very dirty.

"Son," he said, and his breath was vile, "I've got something!" But I did not stay to hear what it was.

It was the horse-doctor who, when new grass worked through the graves at Eastlawn and blue-jays cawed across the bones of "Smith's Folly," ousted Dr. Sloat as Supreme Serpent and took control of the O-R-R. He promised big things—rejuvenation of the Order along ennobling lines, true patriotism and actual charity, the abolition of the mask and a general cleanup of graft and sin. But his song, without the Jones genius for stirring passions, was a sick cat. Perhaps its very piety paralyzed it. A Red Rider without a hood was ridiculously like a devil without horns. Perhaps the *Sphere's* crusade at last bore fruit and the suckers became wise guys. Perhaps the destruction of the Palace and the disappearance of the treasury was too harsh a double blow. Or perhaps America was simply bored with bloodshed and intrigue and bogeys. The war was over—and the aftermath of war. The country was coming into the golden days when Montgomery & Ward at 466½ already was a rainbow in the skies and even the town bully preferred his radio to beating up the neighbors. I have noticed that people are not very patriotic or religious when they are prosperous and secure.

So the O-R-R, as King Cobras discovered the greater rewards of bootlegging and racketeering, slid with the years into the disconsolate position of a preacher without a congregation or a cause. The Order, here and there, kept alive. It still lives, though very feebly.

Yet I do not predict that it is passing to oblivion. The country has come again into new tempers and new times. But yesterday you may have read some imperial python's clarion challenge to Communism—or was it the Japs? Who shall say that, tomorrow, "Cum clab ad Clastra!" will not ring once more across those templed hills?

THE END